365 Animal Stories and Rhymes

Written by: Kath Smith, Gaby Goldsack, Kath Jewitt, Moira Butterfield, Pat Jacobs, Deborah Chancellor, Peter Bently, Karen Hayles, Steve Smallman, Emily Gale, Jillian Harker, Sandy Ransford.

Illustrated by: Alicia Padrón, Steve Whitlow, Amanda Gulliver, Daniel Howarth, Veronica Vasylenko, Dubravka Kolonovic, Lesley Harker, Sanja Rescek, Gavin Scott, Priscilla Lamont, Anna Jones, Kristina Khrin, Jacqueline East, Simon Mendez, Jenny Jones, Caroline Pitcher, John Bendall-Brunello, Andrew Breakspeare, Shelagh McNicholas, Steve Smallman, Adrienne Salgado, Steve Lavis, Mark Marshall, June Goulding, Michelle White.

Every effort has been made to acknowledge the contributors of this book. If we have made any errors, we will be pleased to rectify them in future editions.

Designed by Dynamo Design

This edition published by Parragon Books Ltd in 2014

Parragon Books Ltd
Chartist House
15–17 Trim Street
Bath BA1 1HA, UK
www.parragon.com

ISBN 978-1-4723-7093-8

Printed in China

365 Animal Stories and Rhymes

Bath • New York • Cologne • Melbourne • Delhi
Hong Kong • Shenzhen • Singapore • Amsterdam

Contents

365 Animal Stories and Rhymes

Contents

Contents

Pixie Learns to Jump

Pixie watched the other ponies leap over the brook and sighed. She wished she could jump too, but she was afraid.

"You go on," Pixie's mum called to the rest of the herd. "I'll wait for Pixie."

"Okay," called Pixie's big brother. "Last one to the fallen oak is a donkey!"

"Why can't I jump?" wailed Pixie.

"You can," said her mum gently. "You just need to learn. Try jumping over that little branch over there."

Pixie looked at the branch, took a deep breath, and rushed at it. **Whoops!** She tripped over and fell flat on her nose.

"You need to slow down," smiled her mum, trotting over. "Watch me... Take it steady, don't panic, then glide over."

The next time, Pixie copied her mum and sailed over the branch with ease. She whinnied merrily as she jumped the branch again and again. Then, when she was feeling really brave, she jumped over the brook.

"Last one to the fallen oak is a donkey!" she neighed.

The Singing Dinosaurs

One evening Little Stegosaurus was playing chase in the
forest with Diplodocus and Dryosaurus. Suddenly, he stopped
and looked around. "Uh-oh!" he said. "I think we're lost."

"And it's getting dark," wailed Dryosaurus.

"Don't panic!" cried Diplodocus in a panicky voice.

"I know," said Little Stegosaurus. "Let's sing. Dad always
says that singing makes you feel better!"

The little dinosaurs began to sing their favourite
dinosaur hit. **"Doing the dino stomp!"** they roared.

Their singing echoed through the forest and was soon heard
by Mr and Mrs Stegosaurus, who were busy searching for the
three little dinosaurs. And it wasn't long before it led them to
exactly the right place.

"You were right, Dad," laughed Little Stegosaurus, giving his
parents a big hug. "Singing does make you feel better – but
seeing you and Mum again makes me feel best of all!"

The Fox and the Crow

One day, a crow was flying past an open window when she spotted a tasty piece of cheese on the table. There was no one in the room, so she fluttered in and stole the morsel. Then she flew up into the branches of a nearby tree, and was just about to eat it when a fox appeared.

The fox was particularly fond of cheese and he was determined to steal the crow's prize.

"Good morning, Mistress Crow," he greeted her. "May I say that you are looking especially beautiful today? Your feathers are so glossy, and your eyes are as bright as sparkling jewels!"

The fox hoped that the crow would reply and drop the cheese, but she didn't even thank him for his compliments. So he tried again: "You have such a graceful neck, and your claws are really magnificent. They look like the claws of an eagle."

Still the crow ignored him.

The fox could smell the delicious cheese, and it was making his mouth water. He had to find a way to make the crow drop it. At last he came up with a plan.

"All in all, you are a most beautiful bird," he said. "In fact, if your voice matched your beauty, I would call you the Queen of Birds. Why don't you sing a song for me?"

Now, the crow liked the idea of being addressed as the Queen of Birds by all the other creatures in the woods. She thought that the fox would be very impressed by her loud voice, so she lifted her head and started to caw.

Of course, as soon as she opened her beak the piece of cheese fell **down, down, down** to the ground.

The fox grabbed it in an instant and gobbled it up.

"Thank you," he said. "That was all I wanted. I have to say that you may have a loud voice, but you don't have a very good brain!"

Aesop's moral: Never trust a flatterer.

Hickory Dickory Dock

Hickory dickory dock,
The mouse ran up the clock.
The clock struck one,
The mouse ran down,
Hickory dickory dock.

Cuckoo, Cherry Tree!

Cuckoo, cherry tree!
Catch a bird and give it to me.
Let the tree be high or low,
Let it hail, rain or snow.

Four-and-twenty Tailors

Four-and-twenty tailors went to catch a snail;
The best man among them
Dared not touch her tail.
She put out her horns like a little Jersey cow.
Run, tailors, run, or she'll catch you all now!

If I Were a Bird

If I were a bird I'd sing a song,
And fly about the whole day long.
And when the night came go to rest,
Up in my cosy little nest.

The Magpie

Magpie, magpie,
Flutter and flee,
Turn up your tail,
And good luck come to me.

Haymaking

The maids in the meadow
Are making the hay,
The ducks in the river
Are swimming away.

Why Owls Stare

Once upon a time there lived an owl and a pigeon.
They were friends, but they were great rivals too,
and they were always boasting to one another.

"Owls have much better eyesight than pigeons," the owl
would claim.

"Pigeons are much better at flying," the pigeon would reply.

"Owls have better hearing," the owl would brag.

"Pigeons have prettier feathers," the pigeon would argue.

One morning they were sitting side by side on a branch when
the owl said, "I think there are many more owls than pigeons."

"That can't be right," replied the pigeon. "There are
definitely far more pigeons than owls. There's only one way to
find out. I challenge you to count them!"

"All right," the owl agreed. "We will need a place with plenty
of trees. Let's do it in the Big Wood a week from today. That
will give us time to let everyone know."

During that week the owl and the pigeon flew in
every direction to tell their fellow birds to come to the
Big Wood to be counted.

The day of the count came, and the owls were the first
to arrive. It seemed as if every tree was full
of owls hooting at each other.

16

There were so many, the owls were sure they would
outnumber the pigeons.

Suddenly the sky went dark. Clouds of pigeons were flying
towards the Big Wood. They came from the north, the south,
the east and the west. Soon there was no space left in the trees,
and branches were starting to break under the weight
of all the pigeons.

More and more pigeons came, circling above the wood,
looking for a place to land. By now, the ground was
completely covered with pigeons, too. The owls were wide-
eyed with amazement as they stared at all the pigeons, who
were still arriving by their thousands. The noise of their wings
was deafening, and the owls were getting squashed
and trampled by the ones who had managed to find a perch
in the trees.

"Let's get out of here," the owls hooted to one another, flying
away. But the poor creatures had stared so long and hard at
the pigeons that their eyes stayed stuck wide open – and from
that day on owls always stared, and hid during the day when
the pigeons were nearby, flying only at night.

Teddy Bear, Teddy Bear

Teddy bear, teddy bear,
Turn around.
Teddy bear, teddy bear,
Touch the ground.
Teddy bear, teddy bear,
Climb the stairs.
Teddy bear, teddy bear,
Say your prayers.
Teddy bear, teddy bear,
Turn out the light.
Teddy bear, teddy bear,
Say good night.

One, Two, Three, Four, Five

One, two, three, four, five,
Once I caught a fish alive.
Six, seven, eight, nine, ten,
Then I let it go again.
Why did you let it go?
Because it bit my finger so.
Which finger did it bite?
This little finger on the right.

Goldilocks and the Three Bears

Once there was a beautiful little girl called Goldilocks, with gleaming golden hair. But although she looked like an angel, Goldilocks didn't behave like one. She was often naughty, and didn't do as she was told.

One day, Goldilocks went out to play.

"Stay close to home," her mother reminded her. "Don't go into the forest, or you will get lost."

At first, Goldilocks did as she was told. But then she started to get bored. "Why shouldn't I go into the forest if I want to?" she muttered to herself. "I won't get lost if I stay on the path."

When her mother wasn't looking, Goldilocks skipped across the meadow and into the forest. She had so much fun, she forgot about staying on the path. It wasn't until her tummy began to rumble that she realised she was lost.

"Drat!" she said. "I'm hungry!"

Suddenly, Goldilocks caught a whiff of something yummy.

"Hhhmmm!" she sniffed. "That smells delicious." The smell led Goldilocks

to the door of a small house.
She knocked loudly.
RAT-A-TAT-TAT!
"I don't see anyone," said
Goldilocks, peeking in through the
window. "They must be out."
So she opened the door and
marched right in.

On the kitchen table were three
bowls of sticky, syrupy porridge:
a great big one, a middle-size one
and a teeny-weeny one.

In an instant, Goldilocks dipped a spoon into the biggest
bowl and slurped the porridge hungrily.

"Ouch!" she spluttered. "That's too hot!"

Next she tried the middle-size bowl of porridge. YUCK!
It was much too cold. So Goldilocks dipped her spoon into the
teeny-weeny bowl and tasted it. YUM! It was just right.
She gobbled it all up quickly!

When she had finished licking the syrupy spoon, Goldilocks
looked around the room. There were three comfy chairs by the
fire: a great big one, a middle-size one and a tiny one.

"Just the place for a nap," yawned Goldilocks sleepily.
She flopped down onto the biggest chair.

"Ouch!" she yelled, jumping up. "That's too hard!"

The middle-size chair was even worse. It was much too soft.

So Goldilocks tried the tiny chair. It was very small, but finally she managed to squeeze herself onto the seat. Suddenly, there was a loud SNAP! then CRASH! Goldilocks fell to the floor in a heap of broken chair legs.

Then Goldilocks saw a staircase in the corner of the room. At the top, she found a room with three beds in it: a great big one, a middle-size one and a tiny one.

"I'll just lie down for a little while," Goldilocks decided. So she bounced onto the biggest bed. OOF! It was much too lumpy. Then she bounced onto the middle-size bed. FLUMP! "Too squashy!" she giggled, rolling off.

Goldilocks sat on the tiny bed and tried a little bounce. It was just right, so she lay down. Soon she was fast asleep. She didn't know the owners of the house were coming home.

The owners of the house were a family of bears: a big daddy bear, a middle-size mummy bear and a tiny baby bear! As soon as they got home, the bear family went straight to the table to eat their breakfast...

"Who's been eating my porridge?" growled Daddy Bear.

"And who's been eating my porridge?" growled Mummy Bear.

"At least you've got some left!" cried Baby Bear. "Look! Mine's all gone. Even the spoon is licked clean!"

Daddy Bear looked around the room. "Who's been sitting in my chair?" he growled.

"Who's been sitting in my chair?" growled Mummy Bear.

"At least you've still got a chair!" cried Baby Bear. "Look! Mine's all broken!"

The three bears went upstairs.

"Who's been lying on my bed?" growled Daddy Bear.

"And who's been lying on my bed?" growled Mummy Bear.

"At least there's no one in your bed!" cried Baby Bear.

At that very moment, Goldilocks woke up and saw the three bears. At first she thought she was dreaming. But when the biggest bear growled,

"WHO ARE YOU?"

she knew it wasn't a dream. She leaped up, ran down the stairs, and did not stop until she reached home.

And from that day on, Goldilocks changed her ways. Not only did she look like an angel, but she tried to behave like one, too. Well... most of the time!

Who Lives in a Hole?

Who lives in the hole in the wall of my house?
Can you guess – it's a little brown mouse!

A Swarm of Bees in May

A swarm of bees in May is worth a load of hay.
A swarm of bees in June is worth a silver spoon.
A swarm of bees in July isn't worth a fly.

Old Farmer Giles

Old Farmer Giles,
He went seven miles
With his faithful dog Old Rover;
And his faithful dog Old Rover,
When he came to the stiles,
Took a run and jumped clean over.

If Pigs Could Fly

If pigs could fly
High in the sky,
Where do you think they'd go?
Would they follow a plane
To France or Spain,
Or drift where the wind blows?

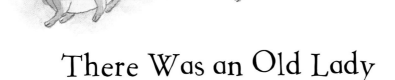

There Was an Old Lady

There was an old lady who swallowed a fly,
I don't know why she swallowed a fly.
Perhaps she'll die!

There Was Once a Fish

There was once a fish. (What more could you wish?)
He lived in the sea. (Where else would he be?)
He was caught on a line. (Whose line if not mine?)
So I brought him to you. (What else should I do?)

I Wish...

I wish I was an elephant,
'Cause it would make me laugh,
To use my nose like a garden hose,
To rinse myself in the bath.

I wish I was a chameleon,
Chameleons are the best.
I'd change my colour and life would be fuller,
'Cause I'd always be well dressed!

I wish I was a dolphin,
A dolphin would be my wish.
Leaping and splashing, I'd be very dashing,
And swim along with the fish.

I wish I was an ostrich,
An ostrich would be grand.
But if I got scared, would I be prepared
To bury my head in the sand?

I wish I had more wishes,
But now my game is through,
I'm happy to be just little old me,
Enjoying a day at the zoo.

Winter Nights

Blow, wind, blow! Drift the flying snow!
Send it twirling, whirling overhead!
There's a bedroom in a tree,
Where, snug as snug can be,
The squirrel nests in his cosy bed.
Shriek, wind, shriek!
Make the branches creak!
Battle with the boughs till break of day!
In a snow cave warm and tight,
Through the icy winter night,
The rabbit sleeps the peaceful hours away.
Call, wind, call! In doorway and in hall!
Straight from the mountain white and wild!
Soft purrs the cat, on her fluffy mat,
And beside her nestles close her furry child.
Scold, wind, scold, so bitter and so bold!
Shake the windows with your tap, tap, tap!
With half-shut, dreamy eyes,
The drowsy baby lies,
Cuddled close in his mother's lap.

Mary Had a Little Lamb

Mary had a little lamb,
Whose fleece was white as snow.
And everywhere that Mary went,
The lamb was sure to go.
It followed her to school one day,
Which was against the rules.
It made the children laugh and play,
To see a lamb at school.
And so the teacher turned it out,
But still it lingered near,
And waited patiently about,
Till Mary did appear.
"Why does the lamb love Mary so?"
The eager children cry.
"Why, Mary loves the lamb, you know,"
The teacher did reply.

Incy Wincy Spider

Incy Wincy Spider
Climbed up the waterspout,
Down came the rain
And washed the spider out.
Out came the sun
And dried up all the rain,
So Incy Wincy Spider
Climbed up the spout again.

Lionel Can Sing!

Lionel was a happy elephant and always singing – but his singing didn't make everyone else happy. It was much too noisy!

"Be quiet!" his friends would roar, every time he sang.

One day, after his friends had yelled back, **"Be quiet!"** particularly loudly, Lionel started to feel really sad.

"What you need is singing lessons," said his friend Mouse. "Let's ask Bluebird."

So Lionel lifted Mouse onto his back and together they went to Bluebird's tree in the jungle.

When Lionel explained the problem, Bluebird was happy to help.

"Breathe in deeply," she told him. "Let your chest fill with air, then blow out through your trunk s...l...o...w...l...y!"

It wasn't long before Lionel was singing as sweetly as a bluebird – but a little more loudly. "I can sing after all," cried Lionel happily. "TOOTLE! TOOT!"

Practice Makes Perfect

One day a sign appeared on the monkey puzzle tree.

"Acrobatic competition at Treetop School this Friday," read Ralph the monkey. "All welcome."

Ralph chattered excitedly. He loved acrobatics.

"I'm going to enter," he informed his mum. "I'll have to practise hard." Then he leaped into the air and did a cartwheel.

"Please do be careful," cried Mum.

But Ralph wasn't listening. He bounced higher and higher, until – ouch! – he landed on his head with a thump.

"Oooo!" groaned Ralph. "I don't think I want to do acrobatics any more."

"Why don't you practise on your bed," suggested Mum. "That way, it won't hurt if you fall."

"What a good idea," cried Ralph.

After that, Ralph practised his tricks every night in his bedroom – rolly-polies, high jumps, handstands and even cartwheels. By the day of the competition, Ralph was able to do them all perfectly. And guess who won the competition? Ralph, of course.

"Practice makes perfect!" grinned Ralph, holding up his trophy.

How the Kangaroo Got His Tail

Once upon a time, a kangaroo and a wombat lived together in a hut. Back then, kangaroos had no tails and wombats had round heads, so they looked different from the way they do today. Although they enjoyed each other's company, the kangaroo liked to sleep outside and the wombat preferred to sleep indoors.

"Why don't you come and sleep outside with me?" the kangaroo would say. "It's lovely to look at the stars and listen to the sound of the wind in the trees."

"It's too cold and it might rain," the wombat would reply. "I'd much rather sleep in the hut in front of the fire."

As winter approached, the wind became stronger and colder.

"I don't mind a bit of wind," the kangaroo told himself as he huddled up next to a tree, trying to keep warm. Then it began

to rain. By the middle of the night the kangaroo felt so frozen, he pushed open the door to the hut and went inside.

"You'll have to sleep in the corner," muttered the sleepy wombat, who was snoozing by the fire. "I don't want you making me all wet."

So the poor kangaroo curled up in the draughty corner, where the rain blew in through a hole in the wall.

In the morning, the kangaroo was cold and grumpy. **"Wake up, you selfish wombat!"** he yelled.

The wombat awoke with a start, then tripped and banged his head on the floor, flattening his forehead.

The kangaroo laughed. "That's what you get for not letting me get warm by the fire. Your flat forehead will be a reminder of how badly you treated me last night!"

The wombat was so angry, he picked up a stick and threw it. The stick bounced off the wall and hit the kangaroo, sticking in his bottom.

"And from now on that will be your tail!" laughed the wombat. "It serves you right!"

And THAT is why wombats have flat foreheads, and kangaroos have long tails.

Merry's Big Wish

Once upon a time there was
a beautiful wooden horse named
Merry who lived on a merry-go-
round on the end of a seaside
pier. But Merry wasn't just an
ordinary wooden horse. He was
very special! Every day people
would come along to pat his

nose and make a wish. And almost always that wish would
come true. For you see, Merry was said to have come from a
magical land far away.

Merry loved giving rides to all the little children, and he loved
making wishes come true. But Merry had a wish of his own.
He wished he were real, so that he could gallop across the soft
sand and splash through gentle waves on the seashore.

One night, when everyone had gone home for the day, Merry
heard a neigh and a beautiful white mare appeared.

"Come with me," called the mare.

"I can't," replied Merry.
"I'm not real."

"Anything is
possible," said the
mare, blowing
softly on Merry's
well-rubbed nose.

Suddenly a strange feeling came over Merry. His nose began to tingle and his legs began to twitch. Then he kicked his legs into the air and he was free. He raced after the white mare and splashed through the waves.

"Neigghhh!" cried Merry, as he and the white mare galloped on and on through the night. They didn't stop until they came to a faraway land full of snowy white horses.

"Where are we?" asked Merry.

"This is your home," replied the white mare. "The land where you came from. And all these horses are your brothers and sisters. From now on you will live here with us."

"But what about the merry-go-round and all the little children? And what about the wishes?"

"Don't worry," replied the white mare. "You can work on the merry-go-round each day, then return home each night."

"Neigghhh!" squealed Merry, tossing his mane into the air. "Now I am the happiest horse in the world."

My Little Kitten

My little kitten has such soft fur,
I love it so much when she lets me stroke her,
She loves to play with a ball of wool,
And together we watch it roll, tumble and pull.

A Green Frog

Said the little green frog,
As he sat on a log,
"Nobody really likes me."
A duck came along,
And said, "You are wrong."
And gobbled him up for tea.

A Wise Old Owl

A wise old owl lived in an oak,
The more he saw, the less he spoke.
The less he spoke, the more he heard.
Why can't we all be like that wise old bird?

Sowing Corn

One for the mouse,
One for the crow,
One to rot,
One to grow.

A Horse and Cart

A horse and cart
Had Billy Smart,
To play with when it pleased him;
The cart he'd load
By the side of the road,
And be happy if no one teased him.

An Elephant

When people call this beast to mind
They marvel more and more
At such a little tail behind
So large a trunk before.

The Fox and Grapes

One summer day, a fox was walking through a field when he saw a bunch of juicy grapes dangling high above his head.

"I wish I could have some of those to quench my thirst," he said to himself – but the grapes were out of reach.

The fox stood on his back legs and stretched his neck as far as he could, but the grapes were still too high up. He took several steps backwards, ran towards the grapevine and took a giant leap... **but he missed them!**

So the fox tried again from the other direction. He ran as fast as he could and sprang into the air... but he missed them once more. Determined to get the delicious grapes, the fox jumped again and again and again. Now he was even hotter and thirstier than before – and he still hadn't managed to reach a single grape!

Finally, the fox looked at the grapes with disgust.

"I don't know why I'm wasting my time trying to get those horrible grapes," he said. "I'm sure they taste really sour!"

Aesop's moral: If someone can't get something, they pretend it is not worth having.

Dog and His Reflection

One day, a hungry dog was passing a butcher shop when
he spotted a juicy steak lying on the counter. The dog's mouth
watered at the sight, so he waited until the butcher went out
to the back of the shop, then he ran in and stole it.

On his way home, the dog crossed a narrow bridge over
a river. As he looked down into the water he saw another dog
looking up at him. This dog was also carrying a piece of meat,
and it looked even bigger than the one he already had!

"I want that one!" thought the greedy dog, so he dropped his
own steak into the water and jumped into the river to steal it.

But as he reached out to snatch the prize in his jaws, the steak
disappeared, and the greedy dog's jaws bit on nothing more
than water. He had been fooled by his own reflection – and
was left with nothing to eat at all!

Aesop's moral: It doesn't pay to be greedy.

Three Grey Geese

Three grey geese
In a green field grazing,
Grey were the geese
And green was the grazing.

Grey were the geese,
Green was the grazing,
That's my tale.
Isn't that amazing!

(Repeat the rhyme as fast as you can.)

A Nutty Adventure

Paddy the squirrel was busy scurrying around the forest floor, gathering nuts for his winter store. Then, when he was sure nobody was looking, he pushed each one into his secret hidey-hole in the Giant Beech.

It was hard work, and by noon Paddy decided to take a break. He crept back to the Giant Beech and peeped into the hole to see how many nuts he had collected. You can imagine his horror when he saw that the hidey-hole was empty. All the nuts were gone!

"Someone's stolen my hoard," he shouted angrily. He was so loud, his friends came out to see what was wrong.

"You think that's bad," cried Rabbit, who was rubbing his head. "Someone has been dropping nuts on my head. I've just had to sweep a whole heap out of my door."

Suddenly Badger began to laugh. He knew exactly what had happened. Paddy had been putting his nuts through Rabbit's window!

When Badger explained, Paddy and Rabbit began to chuckle.

"What a nutty adventure," said Paddy.

The Hermit Crab

The hermit crab's a nervous chap,
He wears his home upon his back,
He's often shy, and likes to hide.
If he's scared, he pops inside.
Two beady eyes look all about,
And when it's safe he creeps back out.

Five Teddy Bears

Five teddy bears came out one night,
To dance beneath the pale moonlight,
And count the stars above their head,
(When little bears should be in bed),
Until the sun came up, and then...
The naughty bears crept home again.

Three Little Kittens

Three little kittens,
They lost their mittens,
And they began to cry,
"Oh, Mother dear,
We sadly fear
That we have lost our mittens."
"What! Lost your mittens,
You naughty kittens!
Then you shall have no pie.
Mee-ow, mee-ow, mee-ow, mee-ow.
No, you shall have no pie."
The three little kittens,
They found their mittens,
And they began to cry,
"Oh, Mother dear,
See here, see here,
Our mittens we have found."
"Put on your mittens
You silly kittens!
Then you shall have some pie."
"Purr, purr, purr, purr,
Oh, let us have some pie."

The three little kittens
Put on their mittens,
And soon ate up the pie;
"Oh, Mother dear,
We greatly fear
Our mittens we have soiled."
"What! Soiled your mittens,
You naughty kittens!"
Then they began to sigh,
"Mee-ow, mee-ow, mee-ow, mee-ow."
Then they began to sigh.

The three little kittens,
They washed their mittens,
And hung them out to dry;
"Oh, Mother dear,
Do you not hear
That we have washed our mittens."
"What! Washed your mittens,
Then you're good kittens,
But I smell a rat close by!"
"Mee-ow, mee-ow, mee-ow, mee-ow.
We smell a rat close by."

The Turtle's Race With the Bear

One day, a bear was walking near a frozen pond when he spotted a turtle's head sticking out of a hole in the ice.

"Good morning, slow creature," the bear called.

"Why are you calling me slow?" the turtle asked.

"Everyone knows you are the slowest of all the animals," the bear declared. "Anyone could beat you."

"Well let's find out," the turtle said. "Let's have a race."

The bear snorted with laughter at the thought that he could be beaten by a turtle, and he agreed to race the following morning. Soon after sunrise the turtle and the bear met at the pond. Animals had come from miles around to watch the race.

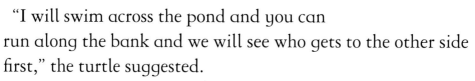

"I will swim across the pond and you can run along the bank and we will see who gets to the other side first," the turtle suggested.

"But how?" the bear asked. "The pond is covered in ice."

"I will make holes in the ice. Each time I reach a hole I will stick my head out," the turtle explained.

The bear and the turtle took up their positions, the bear on the bank and the turtle in the water, and when a hare gave the signal, the race began. Clouds of snow flew up from the bear's feet as he sped away. Meanwhile, the turtle ducked under the ice and, in no time at all, his head appeared at the next hole.

"Come on, bear!" he shouted, "I'm in front of you already!"

The bear ran even faster, but seconds later, the turtle's head popped up from the next hole. No matter how fast the bear ran, he couldn't keep up with the turtle.

By the time the bear finished the race, he could hardly walk, but the turtle was there waiting for him.

The bear was so exhausted and embarrassed at having been beaten that he staggered back home and didn't come out again until spring.

Once the bear and the other animals had left the pond, the turtle tapped on the ice and turtle heads popped up in all the holes in the ice. They belonged to the turtle's family, who all looked just like him.

"We've taught that bear a lesson," the turtle said. "He won't call us slow again!" And ever since then, the bear has slept through the winter until spring arrives.

Old MacDonald

Old MacDonald had a farm,
Ee-i-ee-i-o,
And on his farm he had a duck,
Ee-i-ee-i-o,
With a quack-quack here,
And a quack-quack there,
Here a quack, there a quack,
Everywhere a quack-quack,
Old MacDonald had a farm,
Ee-i-ee-i-o.

Old MacDonald had a farm,
Ee-i-ee-i-o,
And on his farm he had a pig,
Ee-i-ee-i-o,
With an oink-oink here,
And an oink-oink there,
Here an oink, there an oink,
Everywhere an oink-oink,
Old MacDonald had a farm,
Ee-i-ee-i-o.

*(Continue the rhyme, adding in a different
animal and its noise each time.)*

Five Little Monkeys

Five little monkeys jumping on the bed,
One fell off and bumped his head.
Mamma called the doctor,
And the doctor said,
"No more monkeys jumping on the bed."

*(Repeat the rhyme, counting down
by one monkey each time.)*

Tiny Bear

Tiny Bear was a very curious bear, who was always asking lots of questions: "Why is the sky blue?" "Where does the night go?" "How do worms wiggle?"

"Goodness!" Daddy would laugh. "So many questions!" But, of course, he and Mummy Bear always did their best to give Tiny Bear an answer. Knowing the right answer wasn't always easy, though.

One day, the Bear family was strolling through the forest when Tiny Bear had a funny thought.

"What does the world look like upside down?" he asked.

Mummy and Daddy Bear looked at each other and smiled.

"I can't really tell you!" laughed Mummy Bear. "You are going to have to answer that question for yourself!"

"But how?" asked Tiny Bear.

"I'll show you as soon as we get home," replied Mummy Bear.

Tiny Bear ran home as fast as he could. "Hurry up," he cried. "I want to know what the world looks like upside down."

"Right," panted Mummy Bear. "Stand up straight and

stretch your arms up above your head."

"What's that got to do with what the world looks like upside down?" laughed Tiny Bear.

"You'll see in a minute," smiled Mummy Bear. "Point your right foot in front of you, and fall forwards until your hands touch the ground. Then kick your legs into the air and try to hold your legs up straight."

"But I'll fall," squealed Tiny Bear.

"Don't worry," said Mummy Bear. "I'll hold your legs."

Tiny Bear did as Mummy Bear instructed, and could soon do a handstand all by himself.

"What does the world looks like now?" asked Mummy Bear.

"All topsy turvy," laughed Tiny Bear. "This is fun! Why don't you do a handstand and see for yourself?"

"All right," laughed Mummy Bear. "But Daddy Bear will have to do one, too."

Birds of a Feather

Birds of a feather flock together.
And so will pigs and swine.
Rats and mice will have their choice,
And so will I have mine.

Three Blind Mice

Three blind mice, three blind mice,
See how they run, see how they run!
They all ran after the farmer's wife,
Who cut off their tails with a carving knife.
Did you ever see such a thing in your life
As three blind mice?

Down With the Lambs

Down with the lambs,
Up with the lark,
Run to bed children,
Before it gets dark.

Brown Owl

The Brown Owl sits in the ivy-bush,
And she looketh wondrous wise,
With a horny beak beneath her cowl,
And a pair of large round eyes.

Dandy

I had a dog and his name was Dandy,
His tail was long and his legs were bandy,
His eyes were brown and his coat was sandy,
The best in the world was my dog Dandy.

Little Miss Muffet

Little Miss Muffet
Sat on a tuffet,
Eating her curds and whey.
Along came a spider,
Who sat down beside her
And frightened Miss Muffet away.

The Vain Crow

Once upon a time, a crow was flying far from home when he saw a pair of peacocks in a beautiful garden. The crow had never seen such colourful feathers, so he flew down and asked the pair what kind of birds they were.

"We're peacocks," they said proudly, and strutted up and down displaying their magnificent tails.

The crow flew away feeling ashamed of his dull, black feathers. Every time he caught sight of his reflection, he remembered the peacocks and their fabulous blue-green plumage. How he wished he looked like them!

One day the crow spotted a familiar-looking feather on the ground. It must have fallen from a peacock's tail. The crow picked it up and took it back to his nest. The next day he returned to the same place and found another feather. Day after day, the crow went back until he had collected seven fabulous tail feathers.

The crow stuck the peacock feathers to his own black tail and strutted back and forth in front of the other crows, waiting for them to admire him, just as he had admired the peacocks. But instead of being impressed, the other crows just laughed at him and told him he looked ridiculous.

"I don't care. I don't belong with you boring black crows," the vain crow told the rest of the flock. "I'm going to join the peacocks in their beautiful garden."

So the crow flew back to the garden and landed among the peacocks and peahens. He was sure they would welcome him, but the peacocks and peahens knew right away that he was an impostor.

"You're not one of us!" they called. Then they plucked out his borrowed feathers and started to peck him until he had no choice but to fly back home.

At last the crow realised there was no point in pretending to be something that he was not, and he was looking forward to getting back home. But when he rejoined the other crows, they drove him away. "You're not one of us!" they cawed.

So the vain crow flew away sadly, alone, and all because he was not satisfied with his appearance.

Aesop's moral: Be happy with who you are.

Five Little Ducks

Five little ducks went out one day,
Over the hills and far away.
Mama Duck said, "Quack, quack, quack!"
but only four little ducks came waddling back...

Four little ducks went out one day,
Over the hills and far away.
Mama Duck said, "Quack, quack, quack!"
but only three little ducks came waddling back...

Three little ducks went out one day,
Over the hills and far away.
Mama Duck said, "Quack, quack, quack!"
but only two little ducks came waddling back...

Two little ducks went out one day,
Over the hills and far away.
Mama Duck said, "Quack, quack, quack!"
but only one little duck came waddling back...

One little duck went out one day,
Over the hills and far away.
Mama Duck said, "Quack, quack, quack!"
but no little ducks came waddling back...

No little ducks went out one day,
Over the hills and far away.
Mama Duck said, "Quack, quack, quack!"
and five little ducks came waddling back.

Daisy's Big Adventure

Once upon a time there was a marmalade kitten called Daisy who belonged to a little boy named Charlie. Daisy was a very happy little kitten. When she wasn't having fun in the garden, she spent her days playing in Charlie's bedroom. She loved playing with Charlie's toys and knew every one of them by name. And after a hard day's playing, Daisy would curl up and go to sleep on Charlie's bed.

One morning Daisy awoke to find something new sitting on Charlie's bedroom floor. It was a big, square, wooden thing.

"What can it be?" wondered Daisy. She sniffed the "thing" gingerly and prodded it with her paw. "Maybe it's a new place for me to sleep," she thought. And she leaped inside to try it out. But she leaped out again immediately. The "thing" was full of tiny people. They were dressed in fine clothes and looked very important. One of them was even riding a horse!

"Who are they and where have they come from?" she wondered. She hid behind the jack-in-the-box and watched to see what they would do. Daisy waited and waited, but the tiny people did not move. Even the horse stayed perfectly still.

"How strange," thought Daisy. She crept out from her hiding place and gave one of the people a nudge. The poor fellow fell to the ground and didn't move.

"I am sorry," she meowed. "I hope I haven't hurt you."

Just then, Charlie woke up. When he heard Daisy meowing he jumped out of bed and picked her up.

"What are you doing?" he laughed, giving her a hug. "Are you playing with my new castle and toy soldiers?"

"Ahhh," thought Daisy. "So that's why they don't move. They're toys!"

From that day on, the castle became Daisy's favourite toy. She liked nothing better than playing soldiers and kittens. But the game she enjoyed best was knights and dragons – with Daisy as the dragon, of course.

Mrs Hen

Chook, chook, chook, chook, chook,
Good morning, Mrs Hen.
How many chickens have you got?
Madam, I've got ten.
Four of them are yellow,
And four of them are brown,
And two of them are speckled red,
The nicest in the town.

Gee up, Horsey

Gee up, horsey,
Off we go,
Clippety cloppety,
Nice and slow.
Clippety cloppety,
Down the lane,
All the way,
Then back again.

The Donkey and the Load of Salt

One day, a merchant went to collect some sacks of salt from the seashore. He piled the sacks onto the back of his donkey and they started to make their way home.

The donkey struggled to carry the heavy load, and as he crossed a shallow river he slipped on the wet stones. SPLOSH! The sacks tumbled into the water. By the time the man had picked them up, most of the salt had been washed away.

"That's better!" thought the donkey, as the man reloaded the half-empty sacks onto his back. And he trotted on happily down the road.

The following day, the merchant went back to the seashore to get more salt and loaded up the donkey once again.

Now, the donkey was very annoyed at having to carry another heavy load, so when they reached the river on their

way home, he remembered what had happened the day before and pretended to slip. SPLASH! The sacks of salt fell into the water.

By the time the man had hauled them out, the sacks were half empty again, much to the donkey's delight.

The merchant, who was no fool, soon guessed that the donkey had slipped on purpose this time, and he was very angry. So he came up with a plan to teach the lazy creature a lesson.

The next day, he took the donkey to the seashore again, but this time he loaded two large baskets of sponges onto his back. Of course, the sponges were very light, but by the time they reached the river, the rough baskets were beginning to scratch the donkey's shoulders.

"I know, I'll pretend to slip again," thought the crafty creature – and WHOOPS! – he tipped the sponges into the river.

To the donkey's surprise, the merchant did not get angry. He just picked up the sponges and put them back in the baskets.

"Oh, no!" groaned the donkey, as the baskets filled up. The water-soaked sponges were so heavy! He had no choice but to struggle on home, carrying a load ten times heavier than before.

Aesop's moral: One solution does not fit all problems.

A Farmer Went Trotting

A farmer went trotting upon his grey mare,
Bumpety, bumpety, bump!
With his daughter behind so rosy and fair,
Lumpety, lumpety, lump!
A raven cried, "Croak!" They went tumbling down,
Bumpety, bumpety, bump!
The mare broke her knees and the farmer his crown,
Lumpety, lumpety, lump!
The mischievous raven flew laughing away,
Bumpety, bumpety, bump!
And vowed he would serve them the same the next day,
Lumpety, lumpety, lump!

Lark-bird

Lark-bird, lark-bird, soaring high,
Are you never weary
When you reach the empty sky?
Are the clouds not dreary?
Don't you sometimes long to be
A silent goldfish in the sea?
Goldfish, goldfish, diving deep,
Are you never sad, say
When you feel the cold waves creep?
Are you really glad, say?
Don't you sometimes long to sing
And be a lark-bird on the wing?

Brown Bird

Little brown bird,
Where do you live?
"Up on yonder wood, sir,
On a hazel twig."

Charley Warley

Charley Warley had a cow,
Black and white about the brow;
Open the gate and let her through,
Charley Warley's old cow.

Cock Crow

The cock's on the woodpile
Blowing his horn,
The bull's in the barn
A-threshing the corn.

Cats and Dogs

Hoddley, poddley, puddle and fogs,
Cats are to marry the poodle dogs;
Cats in blue jackets and dogs in red hats,
What will become of the mice and the rats?

Feathers

Cackle, cackle, Mother Goose,
Have you any feathers loose?
"Truly have I, pretty fellow,
Half enough to fill a pillow.
Here are quills, take one or two,
And down to make a bed for you."

Fishes Swim

Fishes swim in water clear,
Birds fly up into the air,
Serpents creep along the ground,
Boys and girls run round and round.

The Velveteen Rabbit

Once upon a time, there was a Velveteen Rabbit made from soft fur, with ears lined with pink satin. When he was given to the Boy on Christmas morning, he was the best present.

At first, the Boy thought the Velveteen Rabbit was wonderful, but then he put him away in the cupboard.

"What is **real?**" the Velveteen Rabbit asked the toys in the cupboard one day.

"It's what you become when a child really loves you," explained a hobbyhorse. "I was made real a long time ago by the Boy's uncle. It can take a very long time. By the time you are real some of your fur has dropped out. But it doesn't matter, because once you are real you can't be ugly."

One night, when Nanny was putting the Boy to bed she couldn't find his favourite toy. So she grabbed the Velveteen Rabbit by his ear.

"Here, take your old bunny!" she said. And from that night on, the Velveteen Rabbit slept with the Boy.

At first it was a bit uncomfortable. The Boy would hug him

so tightly that the Velveteen Rabbit could hardly breathe. But soon he grew to love sleeping with the Boy. And when the Boy went to sleep, the Rabbit would snuggle down and dream about becoming real.

The Velveteen Rabbit went wherever the Boy went. He had rides in the wheelbarrow, and picnics on the grass. He was so happy that he didn't notice that his fur was getting shabby.

One day, the Boy left the Rabbit on the lawn. At bedtime, Nanny came to fetch the Rabbit because the Boy couldn't go to sleep without him.

"Imagine all that fuss about a toy," said Nanny.

"He isn't a toy. He's real!" cried the Boy.

When the Rabbit heard these words he was filled with joy! He was real! The Boy himself had said so.

Late one afternoon, the Boy left the Rabbit in the woods while he went to pick some flowers. Suddenly, two strange creatures appeared. They looked like the Velveteen Rabbit, but they were very fluffy. They were wild rabbits.

"Why don't you come and play with us?" one of them asked.

"I don't want to," said the Velveteen Rabbit. He didn't want to tell them that he couldn't move. But all the time he was longing to dance like them.

One of the wild rabbits danced

so close to the Velveteen Rabbit that it brushed against his ear. Then he wrinkled up his nose and jumped backwards.

"He doesn't smell right," the wild rabbit cried. "He isn't a rabbit at all! He isn't **real!"**

"I am real," said the Velveteen Rabbit. "The Boy said so."

Just then, the Boy ran past and the wild rabbits disappeared.

"Come back and play!" called the Velveteen Rabbit. But there was no answer. Finally, the Boy took him home.

A few days later, the Boy fell ill. Nanny and a doctor fussed around his bed. No one took any notice of the Velveteen Rabbit snuggled beneath the blankets.

Then, little by little, the Boy got better. The Rabbit listened to Nanny and the doctor talk. They were going to take the Boy to the seaside.

"Hurrah!" thought the Rabbit, who couldn't wait to go, too.

But the Velveteen Rabbit was put into a sack and carried to the bottom of the garden, ready to be put on the bonfire.

That night, the Boy slept with a new toy for company. Meanwhile, at the bottom of the garden, the Velveteen Rabbit was feeling lonely and cold. He wiggled until his head poked out of the sack and looked around. He remembered all the fun he had with the Boy. He thought about the wise hobbyhorse.

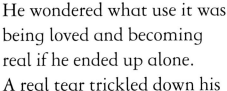

He wondered what use it was being loved and becoming real if he ended up alone. A real tear trickled down his velvet cheek onto the ground.

Then a strange thing happened. A tiny flower sprouted out of the ground. The petals opened, and out flew a tiny fairy.

"Little Rabbit," she said, "I am the Nursery Fairy. When toys are old and worn and children don't need them anymore, I take them away and make them real."

"Wasn't I real before?" asked the Rabbit.

"You were **real** to the Boy," the Fairy said, "But now you shall be **real** to everyone."

The Fairy caught hold of the Velveteen Rabbit and flew with him into the woods where the wild rabbits were playing.

"I've brought you a new playmate," said the Fairy. And she put the Velveteen Rabbit down on the grass.

The little rabbit didn't know what to do. Then something tickled his face and, before he knew what he was doing, he lifted his leg to scratch his nose. He could move! The little rabbit jumped into the air with joy.

He was **real** at last.

Sweet Sparrow

Come hither, sweet sparrow,
And be not afraid,
I would not hurt even a feather;
Come hither, sweet sparrow,
And pick up some bread,
To feed you this very cold weather.
I don't mean to frighten you,
Poor little thing,
The kitty cat is not behind me;
So hop about pretty,
And drop down your wing,
And pick up some crumbs,
And don't mind me.

Guinea-pig

Once there was a guinea-pig,
He was not small, he was not big.
He always walked upon his feet,
His favourite food was greens to eat.
Sometimes he tried to run away,
Sometimes he would stay to play.
And when he ran, he ran so fast,
You barely saw him running past.
He sometimes called quite noisily,
And often squeaked "Hello!" to me.

The Lion and the Mouse

One day, a lion was fast asleep in his den when he was woken by something running across his face. The lion lazily opened one eye and was surprised to see a little mouse right in front of his nose. As fast as lightning, the lion's paw shot out and caught the mouse.

"How dare you run across the face of the king of beasts!" the lion roared. "You will pay for that with your life!"

The lion opened his enormous mouth and was just about to swallow the mouse, when he heard the creature squeaking.

"Please don't eat me, sir," the mouse pleaded. "If you forgive me and let me go, I will do something for you one day, to repay your kindness."

The lion laughed and laughed at the thought that a creature as small and unimportant as a mouse could ever do anything to help the king of beasts.

"You repay me?" the lion spluttered. "I can't imagine that."

But, because the lion had just eaten a big meal and he found the mouse's plea so funny, he let the little creature go.

Some time later, the lion was stalking a zebra when he became caught in a net that had been laid on the ground by hunters. The lion tried to free himself, but the more he struggled, the more he got tangled in the ropes. Soon, he was too exhausted to struggle anymore, or even roar for help.

The lion had almost given up hope of ever escaping, when who should come by but the little mouse he had let go earlier.

"Let me help you," squeaked the little mouse, climbing onto the lion's shoulder. And he began to nibble through the ropes with his sharp teeth. Soon he had bitten through most of the knots, and the lion wriggled free.

Before running off, the lion thanked the little mouse.

"I am very grateful to you, my friend," he said. "You have taught me an important lesson: no act of kindness is wasted, however small it may be."

Aesop's moral: Little friends can turn out to be great friends.

The Fox and the Stork

Once upon a time a fox decided to play a trick on his neighbour, the stork.

"Would you like to come and have supper with me?" he asked her one morning.

The stork was surprised by the invitation, because the fox had never been friendly to her before, but she happily accepted. He looked like a well-fed beast, and she was sure he would provide her with a good meal.

Every now and then, through the day, the stork caught the mouth-watering smell of the soup that the fox was preparing. By the time she arrived at his home she was feeling very hungry – which was exactly what the fox wanted.

"Enjoy your meal," said the crafty fox, ladling the soup into a shallow bowl. Of course, the fox was able to lap his up easily, but the stork could only dip the tip of her bill

into the soup. She wasn't able to drink a single drop!

"Mmm, that was delicious," said the fox when he had slurped up the soup. "I see you don't have much of an appetite, so I will have yours, too."

The poor stork went home feeling hungrier than ever and was determined to take her revenge on the sly fox for playing such a mean trick. So the following week, she went to see him.

"Thank you for inviting me to supper last week," she said. "Now I would like to return the favour. Please come and dine with me this evening."

The fox was a little suspicious that the stork might want to get her own back, but he didn't see how she could possibly play a trick on him. After all, he was known for his cunning, and very few creatures had ever managed to outwit him.

All day long the fox looked forward to his supper, and by the evening he was very hungry. As he approached the stork's home he caught the appetising aroma of a fish stew and started to lick his lips.

But when the stork served the stew it was in a tall pot with a very narrow neck. The stork could reach the food easily with her long bill, but the fox could only lick the rim of the pot and sniff the tempting smell. Much as he didn't want to, the fox had to admit he had been outsmarted – and went home with an empty stomach!

Aesop's moral: One bad turn deserves another.

Little Spiders

Little spiders work and spin...
Webs to catch their dinner in.

A Little Boy Went into the Barn

A little boy went into the barn,
And lay down on some hay.
An owl came out and flew about,
And the little boy ran away.

When the Cuckoo Comes

When the cuckoo comes to the bare thorn,
Sell your cow and buy your corn.

If I Had a Donkey

If I had a donkey that wouldn't go.
Would I beat him? Oh, no, no.
I'd put him in the barn and give him some corn.
The best little donkey that ever was born.

The Groundhog

If the groundhog sees his shadow,
We will have six more weeks of winter.
If he doesn't see his shadow,
We will have an early spring.

I Had Two Pigeons

I had two pigeons bright and gay,
They flew from me the other day:
What was the reason they did go?
I cannot tell, for I do not know.
Coo-oo, Coo-oo!

The Little White Duck

There's a little white duck (quack)
Sitting in the water.
A little white duck (quack)
Doing what he oughter.
He took a bite of a lily pad,
Flapped his wings and he said,
"I'm glad I'm a little white duck
Sitting in the water.
Quack, quack, quack!"

Muddypaws!

It was a special day for Ben. He had a new puppy!

"I'll teach you all the things I know," said Ben. "But first I need to choose a name for you. I'll need to think hard about it. It has to be just perfect."

"I don't really mind what name you choose, as long as you give me lots of cuddles," thought the puppy.

Ben looked around his bedroom to see if he could find an idea for the perfect puppy name.

"I'll look in my storybook," he said, but none of the names in the book were right.

"I think I'll let you hunt for names," thought the new puppy. "I'd rather look behind that flowerpot."

The little puppy crept over... He sniffed...

... and then he climbed. He didn't mean to knock the flowerpot over, but...

Oops! That's just what he did. He made muddy paw prints everywhere.

"Let's go to the park. I might be able to think of a good name there," said Ben.

"I'd rather look behind that tree,"thought the little puppy. So he ran... and he ran.

He didn't mean to jump in the mud, but... **squelch!** That's just what he did. He made muddy paw prints everywhere.

Ben's neighbours were having a party in their back garden.

"One of the guests might be able to think of a good name for you," said Ben. "Let's go and ask them."

"I'd rather look in the pond," thought the new puppy. So he leaned over... and he leaned over a little bit more. He didn't mean to fall in the pond, but...

splosh! That's just what he did.

He made muddy paw prints everywhere.

"We'd better go home and clean you up," said Ben.

"I'd rather go digging in the garden," thought the new puppy.

So he dug... and he dug... and he dug. This time he found lots of things... a lost ring... an old wrench ... and a toy car that Ben had lost. He didn't mean to bring all that mud indoors, but... **pitter patter**... that's just what he did, all over the kitchen floor. He made muddy paw prints everywhere.

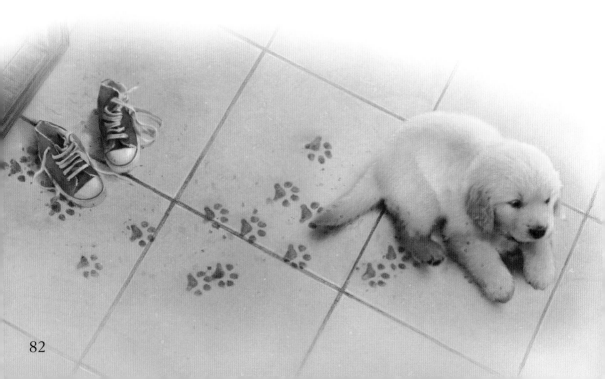

And he didn't mean to find a name for himself at last,
but... guess what? That's *just* what he did!

"You are the muddiest, funniest puppy there ever was.
There's only one name for you," laughed Ben.

Can you guess what it is?

"Muddypaws!"

Just One More Swim!

Big Bear stood up and sniffed the air, then lumbered out towards the water. Her cubs scampered after her, blinking at the dazzling world.

Big Bear padded across the ice. She stopped and dug a hole. She dipped in her paw and scooped out a fish!

The cubs did just what Big Bear did. One dug a hole. The other pounced on the cloud of white, and frightened off the fish. The cubs squabbled. They fought. They tackled each other and tumbled and rolled, over and over in the snow. They ran and raced on their snowshoe paws, and tummy-tobogganed on the ice. But then they stopped and stared.

"What is that?" they asked, gazing at the blue-green water.

Every morning, Big Bear coaxed her cubs a little farther towards the ocean. Then one day, Big Bear and her cubs slowly and carefully made their way to the water's edge. Big Bear gently slid into the icy sea.

"Come back!" squealed the cubs. But Big Bear swam out strongly to an island of ice in the waves.

The cubs waited, shivering on the thin ice. The water rippled.

The cubs patted it – but it just wouldn't stay still. Then they put two paws in… and pulled them right back out again.

Big Bear called to her cubs to swim over to the island. "Come to me across the ocean," she urged. "You can do it! Swim!"

And the cubs did! Under the water they went, twisting and turning in the aquamarine sea. Then they dived down from on high, cutting through the waves, paddling with their paws. They splashed and somersaulted through the icy water. They paddled and swam until Big Bear insisted, "Come out now!"

The cubs pulled their weary bodies onto the ice. Then Big Bear led her cubs to where the juicy blueberries grew. The cubs ate and ate, until their muzzles and paws turned blue.

Big Bear sprawled on her back, enjoying the sunshine on her damp fur. But the cubs had other ideas. And, as they headed back towards the water one more time, Big Bear smiled as she heard their call… **"Just one more swim!"**

Twitching Whiskers

Twitching whiskers,
Big long ears,
Little bobtails
On their rears,
Still as statues,
One, two, three –
Then hippety hoppety,
You can't catch me!

How Many Bottles?

Oink says the pig,
Cluck says the hen,
Honk says the goose,
We can count ten!
Woof says the dog,
Moo says the cow,
Whoops says the cat,
How many bottles now?

Snuggle Up!

Snuggle up, kitten, warm in your bed.
Let moonlit dreams fill your head.
The little bunny curled up tight,
Dreams of carrots every night.
The baby mouse dreams in his nest,
Of cheese, the food that he loves best.
Shut your eyes, kitten, sleep and dream,
Of balls of wool, and bowls of cream.
Mr Moon will guard your bed.
Good night, sleep tight, sleepyhead!

Sammy Snail

Sammy Snail is slowly moving,
See him slide across the grass.
He leaves a silver path behind him,
We all know when he has passed.

Sammy Snail is never worried,
Though he wanders far and wide,
For on his back his house he carries,
And when he's tired he pops inside.

That's Not My Brother!

The ducklings were off for their
very first swim.

Dora cried, "I want to join in!"

"Come on!" called her brother.
"You're always late!"

And he followed the other ducks
under the gate.

"Where's my brother!"
cried Dora.

"Lost your brother?" asked Frog. "I heard a few quacks.
And look! I am sure those are brother-duck tracks!"

So off Dora waddled, with Frog beside her,
till they came to a spot where the path was wider.

"He's here!" Dora cried as she looked up and saw
that the tracks led right up to a big nest of straw.

"That's not my brother!" she cried. "It's Hen!"

"Lost your brother?" smiled Hen, with a chirpy cluck-cluck.
"Those tracks in the straw might just bring you more luck!"

"It's this way!" cried Frog. "Come along, little buddy!"
"Are you sure?" questioned Dora. "It looks kind of muddy."
They heard something squelching behind a big tree,
and Frog said, "That sounds like your brother to me!"
"That's not my brother!" cried Dora. "It's Pig!"
"Lost your brother?" said Pig, in his cool, muddy hollow.
"Look, there are other fresh tracks you can follow!"
The grass was so tall that they kept tripping over
as they followed the tracks through a big field of clover.
"I don't think that these tracks are a duckling's, do you?"
said Dora, as a very loud voice went... "MOO!"

"That's not
my brother!"
cried Dora. "It's Cow!"
"Lost your brother?"
said Cow, as she
chewed on her dinner.
"Try those little
tracks, where the grass
is much thinner."
Dora took Frog on
a piggyback ride...

all the way to the barn, where the tracks led inside.
"Found him!" cried Frog. "He just dashed through the door...
to nibble a few grains of wheat off the floor!"
"That's not my brother!" cried Dora. "It's Mouse!"

"Lost your brother?" squeaked Mouse. "These tracks are ours.
But who made those prints over there by the flowers?"

"He's here in the garden, right under our noses!"
said Frog as they followed the tracks through the roses.

And then the tracks stopped. Frog declared, "Look, his feet!
Your brother is hiding behind that pink sheet!"

"That's not my brother!" cried
Dora. "It's Goat!"

"Lost your
brother?" said
Goat, his mouth
full of sweater.
"If you follow
those tracks to
the trough you'll
do better."

Frog hopped
ahead, then he
gave a great shout.
"Hey, listen!" he
cried. "Who's that
splashing about?"

Dora quacked happily,
"That must be him!
He's in the old water trough, having a swim."

"That's not my brother!" cried Dora. "It's Puppy!"

"Lost your brother?" yapped Puppy. "No need to despair!
I think you should look by the pond over there."

When they got to the pond there were no ducks in sight.

"But look at these prints," Dora said. "Puppy's right!
They're definitely duck tracks, and so are these others,
which means," Dora grinned, "that I've found…

…all my brothers!"

This Old Man

This old man, he played one;
He played knick-knack on a drum.

Chorus:
With a knick-knack, paddy whack,
Give a dog a bone;
This old man came rolling home.

This old man, he played two;
He played knick-knack on my shoe.

Chorus:
With a knick-knack, paddy whack,
Give a dog a bone;
This old man came rolling home.

This old man, he played three;
He played knick-knack on my knee.

Chorus:
With a knick-knack, paddy whack,
Give a dog a bone;
This old man came rolling home.

This old man, he played four;
He played knick-knack on my door.

Chorus:
With a knick-knack, paddy whack,
Give a dog a bone;
This old man came rolling home.

This old man, he played five;
He played knick-knack on my hive.

Sing the chorus!

Eat, Birds, Eat!

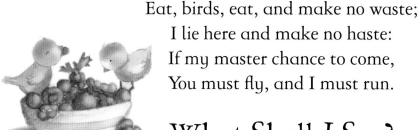

Eat, birds, eat, and make no waste;
I lie here and make no haste:
If my master chance to come,
You must fly, and I must run.

What Shall I See?

See, see! What shall I see?
A horse's head where his tail should be.

I Had a Little Doggy

I had a little doggy that used to sit and beg;
But doggy tumbled down the stairs and broke his little leg.
Oh! Doggy, I will nurse you, and try to make you well,
And you shall have a collar with a little silver bell.

The Evening Is Coming

The evening is coming. The sun sinks to rest.
The birds are all flying straight home to their nests.
"Caw, caw," says the crow as he flies overhead.
"It's time little children were going to bed."
Here comes the pony. His work is all done.
Down through the meadow he takes a good run.
Up go his heels, down goes his head.
It's time little children were going to bed.

The Lion and the Unicorn

The lion and the unicorn
Were fighting for the crown,
The lion beat the unicorn
All around the town.
Some gave them white bread
And some gave them brown,
Some gave them plum cake
And drummed them out of town.

Fishy, Fishy in the Brook

Fishy, fishy in the brook,
Daddy caught him on a hook,
Mummy fried him in a pan,
Johnny ate him like a man.

Dragonfly! Dragonfly!

Dragonfly! Dragonfly! Fly about the brook,
Sting all the naughty boys who for the fishes look;
But let the good boys catch all they can,
And then take them home to be fried in a pan.

Gilbert's Umbrella

One day, Gilbert the mouse was out walking when it started to rain. At first, it was just the occasional drop – pitter patter – but then it began to pour. So Gilbert put up his umbrella and hurried towards his home in the Old Oak Tree.

When he was almost there, Gilbert noticed something very worrying. A river of rain was gushing down the hill – and his cosy, dry home in the Old Oak Tree was on the other side. Before he could decide what to do, a gust of wind blew his umbrella into the water.

"That's it!" cried Gilbert, "I'll use my umbrella as a boat!" Gilbert leaped in and – SWOOSH! – he was swept away. "Oh dear!" he cried. "How can I make it stop?"

The rain river swept Gilbert along, until BUMP – his boat came to a halt. Gilbert laughed. The umbrella had bumped into the roots of the Old Oak Tree. He was home!

"That was fun!" he squeaked as he scrambled out, "but I think I'll stick to walking from now on."

A New Home for Bear

Bear lived all alone on a dusty shelf in the playroom. His boy was grown up now and didn't have time for toys anymore. Then, one day, the boy took him down and dusted him off.

"I think it's time you found a new home," he smiled. "I'm going to put you on the toy table at the school jumble sale."

Bear was very excited. He couldn't wait to find a new child to love. He sat on the toy table and smiled his best smile. But when a little girl reached over to pick up a china doll, she knocked him over and he fell to the ground.

Soon the jumble sale was over and the toy table was put away. No one noticed poor Bear all alone in the grass.

It grew dark and Bear shivered. But he was a brave teddy bear and wasn't afraid of the dark.

In the morning, the sun came up and shone on the pretty flowers. Bear smiled happily – especially when a little girl came by.

"What a happy bear!" she laughed when she saw him. And she picked him up and took him home. She gave him a bath and a ribbon for his neck. At last, Bear had found a new home.

Billy Fox Is Bored

Billy looked out of the kitchen window and sighed. It was so cold and windy that he couldn't go out to play.

He had played with all of his toys. He had finished his favourite book. He had tidied up his bedroom, and had even straightened out his sock drawer. Now there was nothing left to do but peer out of the window and watch the leaves blow by.

"I'm bored," he sighed. "There's nothing to do. Can't I go outside?"

"No," replied Dad gently. "There's a big storm on its way and I don't want you to get caught in it. Why don't we just spend a little time together?"

"But staying inside is boring," moaned Billy Fox. "I want to go out and play with my friends."

"I'm afraid you can't," Dad said firmly. "Do you want to help me make cakes instead? They're your favourite – Woodland Crunch."

"I suppose so," muttered Billy, not sounding at all interested. He watched his dad pour the ingredients into a bowl and sighed wearily.

"Come on," smiled Dad. "Help me mix it all together."

He passed Billy a wooden spoon and soon they were both stirring the bowl energetically.

"**Brrrrrrr!**" went Dad, pretending to be a cement mixer.

"**Brrrrrrr!**" Billy joined in. And soon Billy actually found that, much to his surprise, he was enjoying himself.

Before long, the cakes were ready to go into the hot oven.

"Now we just have to wait for them to cook," said Dad.

"But that's ages!" said Billy.

"Sit back and I'll tell you a story while we wait," suggested Dad. "Once upon a time…"

Dad finished the story just as the cakes came out of the oven. Before long Billy was munching one.

"That was good," cried Billy, licking his lips. "But not as good as spending time with you, Dad. Can we do it again tomorrow?"

The Animal Fair

I went to the animal fair,
All the birds and the beasts were there,
The big baboon by the light of the moon
Was combing his auburn hair.
The monkey bumped the skunk,
And sat on the elephant's trunk;
The elephant sneezed and fell to his knees,
And that was the end of the monkey,
monkey, monkey...

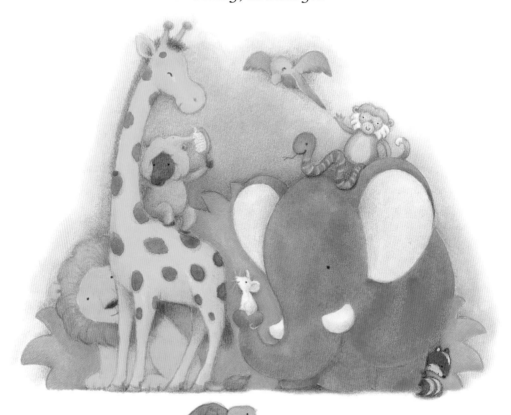

Creature Features

Here is the ostrich straight and tall,
Nodding his head above us all.
Here is the field mouse tiny and small,
Rolling himself into a ball.
Here is the spider scuttling around,
Treading so lightly on the ground.
Here are the birds that fly so high,
Spreading their wings across the sky.
Here are the children fast asleep,
And in the night the owls do peep,
"Toowhit toowhoo, toowhit toowhoo!"

A Horse and a Flea

A horse and a flea and three blind mice,
Were sitting on a corner playing dice.
The horse he slipped and fell on the flea,
"Whoops!" said the flea, "there's a horsie on me!"

A Black-nosed Kitten

A black-nosed kitten will slumber all day,
A white-nosed kitten is ever-glad to play,
A yellow-nosed kitten will answer to your call,
And a grey-nosed kitten I wouldn't have at all!

Pretty Cow

Pretty cow, give me some milk,
And I will give you a gown of silk;
A gown of silk and a silver tee,
If you will give your milk for me.

Bow, Wow, Wow!

Bow, wow, wow! Whose dog art thou?
Little Tom Tinker's dog,
Bow, wow, wow.

The Elephant

The elephant has a trunk for a nose,
And up and down is the way it goes.
He wears such a saggy, baggy hide!
Do you think two elephants would fit inside?

The Rooster

The rooster's on the roof blowing his horn;
The bull's in the barn threshing the corn;
The maids in the meadows are making hay;
The ducks in the river are swimming away.

How Butterflies Came to Be

One day, a long time ago, Elder Brother, the spirit of goodness, was out walking. The summer was over, the sky was blue, and everywhere he looked he saw the colours of autumn.

Soon Elder Brother arrived at a village where the women were grinding corn and children were playing happily together. He sat down feeling very content, as he enjoyed the beautiful autumn colours and the sound of birdsong.

Suddenly, Elder Brother became sad. "It will be winter soon," he thought. "The colourful autumn leaves will shrivel and fall, and the flowers will fade."

Elder Brother tried to think of a way to keep the autumn colours, so that everyone could enjoy them for longer.

Wherever he went, Elder Brother always carried a bag. Now he opened it up and started to fill it with the colours he saw all around him.

He took gold from a ray of sunlight and blue from the sky. He collected shiny black from a woman's hair and white from the cornmeal. He took green from the pine needles, red and yellow from the leaves, and purple and orange from the flowers.

When all the colours were in the bag, Elder Brother shook it. Then he thought of something else. He heard the birds singing and added their songs to the bag.

Elder Brother called the children over.

"I have a surprise for you!" he told them.
"Take this bag and open it."

The children opened the bag, and hundreds of colourful
butterflies flew out. How the children laughed with joy!
The women came over to see the butterflies too, and so did
the men who had been working in the fields. Everyone
stretched out their hands so the butterflies could land
on them, and the butterflies started to sing as they
fluttered around.

The people were delighted, but the birds were angry.
One bird perched on Elder Brother's shoulder.

"Why have you given our songs to the butterflies?"
the bird asked. "We were each given our own
song and now you've given them away to
creatures that have more beautiful colours
than we do."

Elder Brother agreed and apologised to the
birds. He took the songs away from the
butterflies and gave them back to the birds.
And that is how butterflies
came to be – and why
they are silent.

Winnie's Big Egg

It was springtime, and the sun shone brightly over River Farm. Winnie the duck sat on the riverbank and quacked impatiently. She had been sitting on her nest for weeks, but not one of her six eggs had hatched. Winnie shifted around and ruffled her feathers. She turned over her eggs and polished each one. She adored her eggs, but she was beginning to wonder if they would ever hatch. Then, suddenly, there was a CRACK!

Out popped a tiny, fluffy duckling. Winnie was delighted.

Soon the other eggs began to crack, and Winnie was surrounded by five fluffy ducklings. Only the biggest egg remained.

Winnie rolled the big egg beneath her plump chest and

warmed it with her soft feathers. She waited and waited, but the egg didn't hatch.

"Why don't you leave it?" suggested the cow. "You've got five fine little ducklings. That one is obviously no good."

"No," quacked Winnie, wrapping her wings around the egg.

"I don't think that egg even belongs to you," clucked the wise old chicken, who knew a thing or two about eggs. "It's much too big to be a duck egg."

"Yes," neighed the horse. "I've heard about birds leaving their eggs in other birds' nests. It's a terrible thing."

But Winnie just sat on the last egg and waited.

Then, one sunny afternoon, there was a loud CRACK! Winnie quacked with excitement. All the farm animals gathered around to see the new arrival.

"I bet it's a baby goose," whispered the chicken.

"I think it will be a baby swan," neighed the horse.

Everyone held their breath as out popped... two tiny ducklings. It was twins! Winnie quacked with pride. She had always known the big egg was special. Now she had seven perfect little ducklings.

"Come on, boys and girls," she called as she proudly led her babies down to the river.

One Bear Lost

Ten sleepy bears wake from a winter's night.
One wanders out in the early morning light.
Nine scruffy bears wash in a sparkling stream.
One dries off, his fur all fresh and clean.

Eight hungry bears go on a hunt for food.
One wanders off when she smells something good!
Seven silent bears pad softly through the trees.
One sniffs some honey and goes looking for bees.
Six bears have fun in the snow.
One disappears – bottom high, head low.
Five strong bears climb up a slippery slope.
One slides down. She let go of the rope!

Four weary bears take a rest at the top.
One falls over, flippety-flop!
Three lively bears slide down the icy hill.
One stops to rest, calm and still.
Two brave bears paddle, steady and slow.
One gets stranded. Where should he go?
Nine weary bears have gone back home.
But look! One poor bear's left all alone.

One bear lost!

Nine worried bears call out for their friend.
Ten happy bears are back together again.
Ten tired bears are fast asleep in their cosy den.

The Penguin Who Wanted to Sparkle

One moonlit night, Mummy
penguin's egg went CRACK!
A tiny beak appeared, a head,
then two wings and two orange
feet. A fluffy little penguin chick
called Pip hopped out.

"Pretty sparkles!" she squeaked,
as she gazed up at the sparkly stars in the sky. Then Pip saw
a funny fish leap out of the ocean waves – SPLASH! It was
all shiny and sparkly. "I want to sparkle, too," she squeaked.

Soon it began to snow. Pip watched the sparkling snowflakes
floating down. "If I catch some, I can sprinkle them on my
feathers," she thought. "Then I will sparkle, too."

Pip ran around, trying to catch the
snowflakes, but they just melted on
her wings. Then she found a bank of
powdery white snow, twinkling in the
moonlight. "Now I will sparkle!" she
cried, rolling over in the snowy drift.

But the moon disappeared behind
a cloud, and Pip's feathers didn't
sparkle one tiny bit.

"Maybe I can catch a sparkly star,"

thought Pip, jumping up and down. But she couldn't reach one, no matter how hard she tried.

"What are you doing, Pip?" asked the other penguins.

"I'm trying to catch some sparkles," Pip explained.

Just then a friendly whale swam by. "All that jumping and rolling around looks very tiring!" he laughed. "Why don't you come and slide on my back instead?"

Everyone agreed that this was a wonderful idea – even Pip. One by one, the penguins whooshed down the whale's back and landed in the glittering sea. SPLASH! Pip hopped out and shook her wet feathers in the sunshine.

"Look!" cried the other penguins. "You're sparkling all over!"

"So that's how you sparkle," cried Pip, dancing in the snow. "By having fun in the sun. Come on, everyone. Let's do it again!"

I Had a Dog

I had a dog whose name was Buff,
I sent him for a bag of snuff;
He broke the bag and spilled the stuff,
And that was all my penny's worth.

Mary Had a Pretty Bird

Mary had a pretty bird,
With feathers bright and yellow,
Slender legs – upon my word,
He was a pretty fellow.

The sweetest notes he always sang,
Which much delighted Mary;
And near the cage she'd ever sit,
To hear her own canary.

The Wedding

Kitty cat, witty cat, with a white foot,
When is your wedding? I'll come to it.
The bread's to make, and the cake's to bake,
Kitty cat, witty cat, don't be late!

Hark, Hark

Hark, hark, the dogs do bark,
Beggars are coming to town:
Some in rags, some in bags,
And some in velvet gowns.

To Shave a Pig

Barber, barber, shave a pig,
How many hairs to make a wig?
Four and twenty, that's enough,
Give the barber a pinch of snuff.

Pretty John Watts

Pretty John Watts,
We are troubled with rats,
Will you drive them out of the house?
We have mice, too, in plenty,
That feast in the pantry;
But let them stay, and nibble away,
What harm is a little brown mouse?

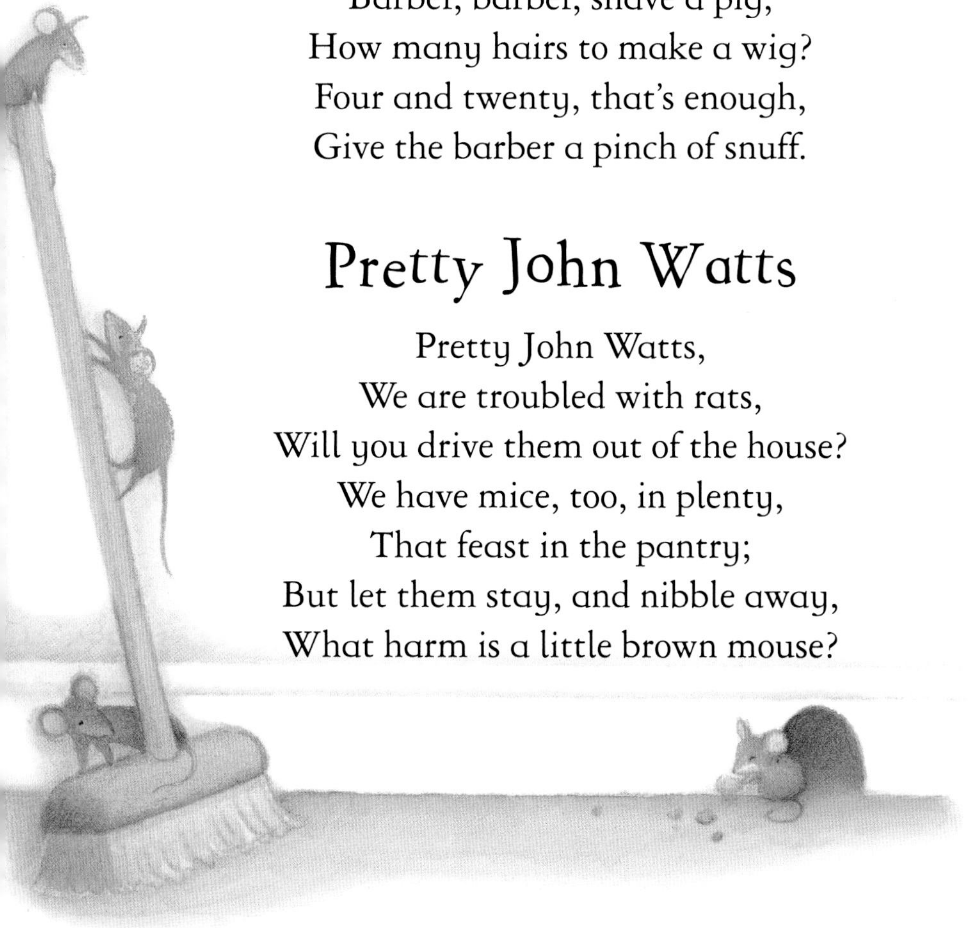

Bunny Burrows

Little bunnies curled up tight,
Sleep in burrows through the night.
Cosy, warm and underground,
In the dark, there's not a sound.
There's just one thing I can't work out –
How do they know when the sun comes out?

Bunnies Come Out to Play

Bunnies all come out to play,
In the sunshine of the day.
They bounce and run and hop around,
Until they hear a scary sound!
At first they freeze – then off they bound,
And dart away beneath the ground.

The Cow

The friendly cow all red and white,
I love with all my heart;
She gives me cream with all her might,
To eat with apple tart.

She wanders lowing here and there,
And yet she cannot stray,
All in the breezy open air,
The pleasant light of day.
And blown by all the winds that pass,
And wet with all the showers,
She walks among the meadow grass,
And eats the meadow flowers.

The Little Turtle

There was a little turtle,
He lived in a box,
He swam in a puddle,
He climbed on the rocks.
He snapped at a mosquito,
He snapped at a flea,
He snapped at a minnow,
And he snapped at me.
He caught the mosquito,
He caught the flea,
He caught the minnow,
But he didn't catch me!

The Squirrel

The winds they did blow,
The leaves they did wag;
Along came a beggar boy,
And put me in his bag.

He took me to London,
A lady me did buy,
Put me in a silver cage,
And hung me up on high.

With apples by the fire,
And nuts for me to crack,
Besides a little feather bed
To rest my little back.

Tiny Tim

There was a little turtle,
His name was Tiny Tim.
I put him in the bathtub,
To see if he could swim.
He drank up all the water,
He ate up all the soap,
And now he is in the bathtub,
With a bubble in his throat.
Bubble, bubble, bubble,
Bubble, bubble, pop!

The Riverbank

The Mole was fed up. "Bother spring cleaning!" he said, and, "BLOW spring cleaning!" He slammed the front door of his underground home behind him and raced up the tunnel that led to the open air.

"This is better than whitewashing!" he said to himself as he skipped across towards a river.

Mole had never seen a river before. He sat on the grass and gazed at the water.

"Hello," called a voice from the bank on the other side of the river. It was the Water Rat.

"Hello, Ratty," said the Mole shyly.

"Hello Mr Mole. Hang on and I'll come across in my boat."

"I've never been in a boat before," said Mole nervously, as he stepped into the boat. "Is it nice?"

"Nice? It's the only thing," said the Water Rat. "Let's make a day of it. We'll have a picnic up the river."

The Mole sighed with contentment and leaned back into the soft cushions. "What lies over THERE?" he asked, waving a paw toward a wood on the far bank of the river.

"Oh, that's the Wild Wood," said Ratty.

"We riverbankers don't go there if we can help it. Ah, here's our picnic spot."

They picnicked on the green banks of a backwater, where the weir filled the air with a soothing murmur of sound.

Suddenly a broad, glistening muzzle with white whiskers broke the surface of the water.

"Mr Otter!" cried Ratty. "Meet my friend Mr Mole."

"Pleased to meet you," said Otter, shaking his wet coat.

There was a rustling from behind them, and a black-and-white animal with a striped head pushed through a hedge.

"Come on, old Badger!" cried Ratty.

"Hurrummph! Company!" grumbled Badger, and turned his back and disappeared.

"That's just like Badger," explained Ratty. "Hates society."

Just then a racing boat, with a short, round figure inside, splashing badly and rolling a good deal, flashed into view.

"There's Toad!" cried the Otter. Ratty waved. Toad waved and then kept on rowing.

"Oh, dear!" chuckled Ratty.

"It looks like Toad's got a new hobby. Once it was sailing. Then it was punting... then houseboating... and now it's a racing rowboat."

The Otter shook his head. "It won't last! Whatever Toad takes up, he tires of it and then he starts on something new."

Just then, a mayfly swerved overhead and then settled on the river. There was a swirl and a CLOOP!, and the mayfly disappeared. And so did Otter, leaving a streak of bubbles.

The picnic party came to an end, and the afternoon sun was setting as Ratty skulled homeward.

"Ratty! Please, I want to row now!" said Mole, and he seized the oars so suddenly that the Rat fell backwards.

"Stop! You'll tip us over!" cried Ratty.

The Mole made a great dig at the water with the oars, missed the surface altogether, and the next moment – SPLOOSH! – the boat capsized!

Oh, dear, how cold the water was, and how very wet it felt! The Mole felt himself sinking down, down, down. How bright and welcome the sun looked as he rose to the surface.

How black his despair as he felt himself sinking again – until
a paw grabbed him by the neck and he was pulled to the bank.

"Now then, Mr Mole, trot up and down the path until you're
warm and dry again," instructed Ratty.

Meanwhile Ratty rescued the boat, the floating oars and the
cushions, before diving for the picnic basket.

It was a limp and sorry Mole that stepped into the boat.
"Oh, Ratty, can you ever forgive me for my stupidity?"

"Goodness me, dear friend," laughed the good-natured Rat.
"What's a little wet to a Water Rat? Don't you think any more
about it – we will always be the best of friends. Look here,
I really think you had better come and stay with me for
a while, and then I'll teach you to row and to swim."

When they got home, Ratty
made a fire in the parlour, and
found a bathrobe and slippers
for the Mole to wear before
seating him in a big armchair
and telling him stories.

It was a very tired and
contented Mole who was taken
upstairs to the best bedroom,
where he lay his head on a soft
pillow and allowed the lap,
lap, lap of the river to send him
off to sleep. What a busy and
wonderful day it had been.

Oh, My Pretty Rooster

Oh, my pretty rooster, oh, my handsome rooster,
I pray you, do not crow before day,
And your comb shall be made of beaten gold,
And your wings of silver grey.

Donkey, Donkey

Donkey, donkey, old and grey,
Open your mouth
And gently bray;
Lift your ears and
Blow your horn;
To wake up the world this sleepy morn.

Down at the Bottom

Down at the bottom
Of the deep blue sea,
I catch fishes,
One, two, three.

Pretty Lambs

May brings flocks of pretty lambs,
Skipping by their fleecy dams.
When the morning sun is red,
The ewe and the lamb go wet to bed.

Ladybird, Ladybird

Ladybird, ladybird, fly away home;
Your house is on fire, your children all gone,
All but one that lies under a stone;
Fly home, ladybird, unless it be gone.

Little Fishes

Little fishes
In the river,
Blowing bubbles,
Fins a-quiver.

The Fox's Tail

One day, a fox was out walking when he heard a loud snap and felt a sudden pain in his tail. The poor fox had been caught in a hunter's trap. He looked behind him and saw that his tail was completely stuck. No matter how much he struggled, he just couldn't free it.

"Help!" he shouted. "Ouch!" he cried. "Owwww!" he howled. But no one came to help him.

At last, the fox pulled and pulled with all his strength and managed to break free, but when he looked back, he saw that his tail had been left behind in the jaws of the trap.

"What will all the other foxes think when they see me?" thought the fox. "They'll all laugh at me. I don't even look like a fox without my tail. It's so embarrassing!"

For days the fox hid away in his den and only came out at night when no one could see him. Then he came up with an idea. He called a meeting of all the foxes in the area.

The foxes gathered in a clearing. Sure enough, as soon as they saw the fox without his tail, they started to laugh.

"I've called you together to tell you about my wonderful discovery," the fox announced, struggling to be heard above their laughter. "Over the years, I've felt that my tail was nothing but a nuisance. It was always getting muddy, and when it rained it got all wet and took ages to dry. It slowed me down when I was hunting, and I never knew what to do with it when I was lying down. So I decided it was time to get rid of it, and I can't tell you how much easier it is to move around without all that extra weight dragging along behind me. I cut my tail off, and I recommend that you all follow my example and do the same."

One of the older foxes stood up. "If I had lost my tail like you, I might have agreed with what you are saying," he said. "But until such a thing happens, I will be very happy to keep my tail, and I am sure everyone else here feels the same."

The other foxes all stood up and proudly waved their tails in the air as they walked away.

Aesop's moral: Do not listen to the advice of someone who is trying to bring you down to their level.

Little Lamb Gets Lost

One day, Little Lamb was grazing in the meadow when Huey, his oldest brother, began to bleat.

"Have you seen how green the grass is on other side of the hedge?" he called. "It looks much juicier than the grass here."

"Baa," agreed Duey, Little Lamb's other brother. "I'm hungry. Let's go over there and eat. Come on, Little Lamb."

Little Lamb wasn't sure he wanted to leave his lovely meadow home.

"But the grass here is delicious," he said. **"It's the best grass in the world!"**

Huey and Duey wouldn't listen. They pushed their way through a hole in the hedge and trotted off. Little Lamb had no choice but to follow.

Huey and Duey trotted on and on, stopping every now and then to munch the grass. They didn't bother to look where they were going. They just sniffed the air and trotted to where the grass smelled sweetest.

Twice they had to paddle across a stream, and once they even pushed through a thick hedge. They didn't let anything get in their way.

At last, as darkness began to fall, they found a place with the juiciest grass of all. They stopped and looked around.

"Where are we?" they baaed. But it was so dark that they couldn't see a thing.

"Ooooh," cried Huey. "We're lost."

"How will we ever find our way back home?" wailed Duey. "We'll have to stay here for the night."

Little Lamb began to cry. "I want to go home," he bleated.

Just then, a cloud shifted in the night sky and the silvery light of the moon shone down on the three sheep. Little Lamb looked around and saw that they were standing beside a big tree.

"I recognise that tree," he said.

"And I recognise that bush over there," added Huey.

"We're back in our meadow," said Duey. "Our noses led us all the way back home."

"Little Lamb was right, after all," laughed Huey. "Our meadow... **has the best grass in the world!**"

"Baaaaa," bleated Little Lamb in agreement. "Shall we have a little bedtime snack?"

What's That Noise?

Little Cub lived on the grassy plain with his mum and sister
Tia. Little Cub loved playing with his mum and Tia, but
sometimes he enjoyed wandering off on his own.

 One day Little Cub decided to explore a new part of the plain.
He prowled through the grass, admiring the acacia
trees and saying hello to everyone who crossed his path.

He was busy introducing himself to a pretty butterfly, when
he heard a loud **grunt**, followed by a big SPLASH!
Something was making lots of noise nearby.

 Little Cub jumped with fright. "Ooooh," he wailed.
"W…w…what was that?" He was so scared that he buried
his head beneath his paws and tried to hide.

 Then a horrible, haunting hoooowl filled the air. Little

covered his ears and quaked with fear. He had never heard anything quite so strange. "Maybe it's a scary, lion-eating monster," he worried.

Just then, Giraffe came ambling through the grass, and he was heading straight for the terrible noise. Little Cub tried to wave to him, but it was no use. Giraffe just kept on going. Suddenly, Little Cub remembered that he was a brave lion. He wasn't scared of anything.

"Wait," he roared bravely. "Let me go first and find out what's making that awful noise."

Giraffe looked surprised – but he let Little Cub lead the way. Little Cub poked his head through the grass, ready to pounce on whatever danger lay ahead.

But he didn't pounce. He didn't even roar. Instead, he began to laugh. It wasn't a scary, lion-eating monster, after all. Can you guess? It was Harold the Hippo singing in the bath!

The Messenger

Bless you, bless you, burnie bee,
Tell me where my true love be;
Be she east, or be she west,
Seek out who she loveth best;
Go and whisper in her ear
That I forever think of her;
Tell her all I have to say
Is about our wedding day.
Burnie bee, no longer stay,
Take to your wings and fly away.

Penguin Parade

Waddle, waddle, waddle,
From side to side,
Penguins go a-walking
Slip, slip, slide, slide.
With a funny jump
The penguins dash
Down to the water,
Splash! Splash! Splash! Splash!
Waddle from the water
With a rock 'n' roll.
Penguins go parading
On a wintry stroll.

The Spider, the Hare and the Moon

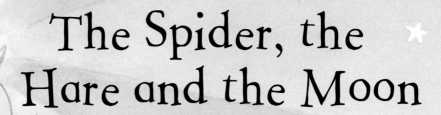

The moon felt very sad. She knew that people on Earth were afraid of the dark, and she wanted to let them know that it was nothing to be scared of. She had no way of speaking to them herself, so she called on her friend the spider.

"Please take a message to everyone on Earth," she said to him. "Tell them that the world will always be in darkness at night, but there is no need to be afraid. I will be here to light their way."

The spider started to climb down the moonbeams to get back down to Earth. On the way, he bumped into the hare.

"Where are you going?" the hare asked.

"The moon has asked me to give an important message to all the people on Earth," the spider explained.

"Oh, you're so slow, it will take you much too long to get there," the hare said. "Let me take the message. I'm much faster than you. I'm sure if the moon said it was important she would want the people to hear it as quickly as possible. Tell me what the message is and I will give it to everyone on Earth."

"Well, I suppose the moon would want the people to hear her message as quickly as possible," the spider agreed. "Tell them the moon said that the world will always be in darkness…"

"Right," said the hare. "Tell the people on Earth that the world will always be in darkness."

And before the spider could finish, the hare had bounded off.

"Wait, wait," the spider shouted after him. "I haven't finished." But the hare had already disappeared.

The spider decided to go back and tell the moon what had happened. Otherwise she would wonder why the people on Earth were still scared.

Meanwhile, on Earth, the hare was busy telling all the people that the world would always be in darkness. And once he had delivered the message, he proudly went back to let the moon know what he had done.

Of course, the moon was furious with the hare – so furious in fact, that she sent him away and wouldn't speak to him ever again.

And the spider? The busy little spider is still trying to carry the moon's message to all the people on Earth as he spins his webs in the corners of our rooms.

ABC

ABC,
Our kitty's up the tree!
And now begins,
With a sneeze and a cough,
To lick her long white stockings off.
No more she'll go into the snow.
Not she, not she, not she!

Magpie

One for sorrow.
Two for joy.
Three for a girl.
Four for a boy.
Five for silver.
Six for gold.
Seven for a secret
Never to be told.
Eight's a wish.
Nine's a kiss.
Ten is a bird you
Must not miss!
Magpie!

The Magic Sky

One icy Arctic night, Lila and Poko the polar bear cubs were getting ready for bed. It was freezing outside, but it was cosy and warm inside their den. The two cubs snuggled down beside their mother and closed their eyes. They were almost asleep, when they heard a noise outside.

"Psst! Lila! Poko!" said a voice. It was their friend Tiki the Arctic hare.

"Come outside! Quickly!" whispered Tiki. "There is something I want to show you. Something very peculiar is happening. I think there must be magic in the air."

"What's going on?" yawned Mother Bear sleepily.

"Something magical is happening," replied Tiki. "I can't describe it. You must come and see for yourself."

"Ah," smiled Mother Bear. "I think I know what it is. Let's all go and take a look together."

The three sleepy polar bears crawled out of their den and padded across the icy snow. Lila and Poko looked around in surprise.

Everything looked so different. The icy landscape was bathed in a strange glow.

"Look up," whispered Tiki.

The polar bear cubs looked up and gasped in amazement. Something very strange was happening in the sky above. It was full of dancing lights, swirling and twirling around above their heads. They all stared in wonder, unable to speak at first.

"It's beautiful!" gasped Poko eventually.

"What's happening?" asked Lila.

"It's the Northern Lights!" said Mother Bear.

"Is it magic?" asked Poko excitedly. "We love magic."

Mother Bear thought for a while and then smiled.

"Yes," she agreed. **"It's the magic of nature!"**

Ride a Cock-horse

Ride a cock-horse to Banbury Cross,
To see a fine lady upon a white horse;
Rings on her fingers and bells on her toes,
And she shall have music wherever she goes.

Miss Jane Had a Bag

Miss Jane had a bag and a mouse was in it;
She opened the bag – he was out in a minute.
The cat saw him jump and ran under the table,
And the dog said, "Catch him, kitty, soon as you're able."

My Little Cow

I had a little cow, hey diddle, ho diddle!
I had a little cow, and I drove it to the stall;
Hey diddle, ho diddle! And there's my song all.

Round About

Round about, round about,
Runs the little hare,
First it runs that way,
Then it runs up there.

Pop Goes the Weasel

Half a pound of tuppenny rice,
Half a pound of treacle.
That's the way the money goes,
Pop! goes the weasel.

Old Mother Goose

Old Mother Goose,
When she wanted to wander,
Would ride through the air
On a very fine gander.

The Three Billy Goats Gruff

Once upon a time, there lived three billy goat brothers. There was a big billy goat, with a great big belly and great big horns. There was a middle-size billy goat, with a middle-size belly and middle-size horns. And there was a little billy goat, with a teeny little belly and teeny little horns.

All three were brave and all had deep, gruff voices, so they called themselves the Billy Goats Gruff.

The three Billy Goats Gruff lived on a hill beside a bubbling river. Across the river was a meadow full of sweet, juicy clover – the goats' favourite food. The goats longed to visit the meadow, but to get there they had to cross a small, rickety wooden bridge.

The Billy Goats Gruff would have happily crossed the small, rickety bridge if it hadn't been for one thing – the meanest, fiercest troll you could possibly imagine lived beneath it. His eyes burned like fire and his warts bristled with thick, dark hairs. He had slimy fangs for teeth and claws as sharp as

razor blades. He was always, always hungry and his favourite food was. . . GOAT!

Few dared cross that bridge, and those that did were never heard of ever again. The Billy Goats Gruff were brave goats, but not stupid, so they stayed away from the bridge and ate the grass in their field. They ate and ate and ate, until one day there was nothing left but dirt.

As the goats looked across the river to the sweet, juicy clover on the other side, their bellies rumbled. Eventually, when they could bear it no more, they decided that they had no other choice but to cross the bridge.

"I'm not scared of that ugly troll," said the little Billy Goat Gruff. So he decided to go first.

The little Billy Goat Gruff's hooves clip-clopped over the bridge. He hadn't gone far when there was a terrifying ROOOAR and the ugly troll leaped out.

"Who's that clip-clopping over my bridge?" roared the troll.

"Only me, the teeny little Billy Goat Gruff," replied the smallest billy goat bravely. "I'm on my way to the meadow to eat some sweet, juicy clover."

"Oh, no, you're not," bellowed the troll. "I'm hungry, and I'm going to gobble you up."

"Please don't do that," replied the brave little Billy Goat

Gruff. "I'm just small and bony. My brother will be coming this way soon. He is far bigger and juicier than me. And he'll make a much better meal."

The troll licked his lips hungrily. He hadn't eaten in a few days but decided he could wait just a little longer if it meant his next meal was even bigger.

"You do look kind of scrawny," he said slowly. "Perhaps I could wait just a little longer for a bigger meal. Now shoo, before I change my mind."

So the little Billy Goat Gruff skipped across the bridge and was soon munching on the sweet, juicy clover on the other side.

Not long afterwards, the middle-size Billy Goat Gruff began clip-clopping his way across the bridge.

"Who's that clip-clopping over my bridge?" snarled the troll.

"Only me, the middle-size Billy Goat Gruff," replied the next billy goat. "I'm on my way to the meadow to eat clover."

"Oh, no you're not," snarled the troll. "I'm going to gobble you up!" And the troll opened his mouth wide, ready.

"Please don't do that," replied the middle-size Billy Goat.

"If you wait a little longer, my big brother will be crossing your bridge. He's got a great big belly and will fill you up in no time at all."

The troll rubbed his huge, round belly greedily. Maybe it wasn't so bad to wait just a bit longer for an even bigger meal.

"Okay," he said finally, "I'll wait for the big billy goat." And he let the middle-size billy goat go.

It wasn't long before he heard a loud clip-clopping sound. The big Billy Goat Gruff was on his way.

"Who's that clip-clopping across my bridge?" roared the troll.

"Just me, the biggest Billy Goat Gruff of all," cried the last billy goat. And before the troll could say a word, he lowered his horns and charged at the troll.

SMACK – the big Billy Goat butted into him and tossed him high into the air. SPLASH! He landed in the water and disappeared.

Then the big Billy Goat Gruff clip-clopped across the bridge to join his brothers in the meadow full of sweet, juicy clover.

And as for the silly old troll? Well, he was never seen ever again!

Frog Goes Exploring

Frog had lived happily on the riverbank for so long that he was friends with everyone – from the smallest minnow to the finest swan. He couldn't wish for a better place to live. But Frog had a secret dream. He dreamed of finding out where the river went. He imagined that it led somewhere exciting – perhaps a great city or an exotic jungle, or maybe a sunny beach.

So one winter, Frog got to work building himself a boat. He sawed and hammered all winter long, and by the spring his boat was ready.

After waving goodbye to all his friends, Frog set off on his great adventure. He hadn't been rowing for long when a head popped out of the river.

"Where are you going?" asked the fish.

"I'm going on a great journey to find the end of the river," Frog explained. And that is exactly what he told everyone he met as he glided slowly along.

All day, Frog rowed down the river, having a wonderful time. The sun shone down, and birds and animals called hello to him. He passed open fields, small villages and great towns. There was so much to see that Frog barely noticed the miles going by, and he never thought about stopping for a rest. On and on he rowed until, suddenly, he stopped with a THUD! The boat had hit dry land, and his journey was over!

Frog looked around with excitement. What fabulous place had he found? But he wasn't greeted by the sight of a grand city or a towering jungle, or even a busy beach. He hadn't arrived at a fabulous place. He had arrived at a small pond.

It wasn't at all what Frog had expected. But he wasn't disappointed. He waved to a friendly bluebird, and called hello to a curious bee. Then he sat back and smiled.

"I've had a wonderful day," he thought. "I've seen lots of lovely things and met so many nice creatures. I guess it's not where you are going but how you get there that is most important!"

The Cowardly Lion

Once upon a time there was a lion called Sabre. Sabre looked just like other lions. He had a big shaggy mane, huge powerful claws, and teeth like daggers. And just like other lions, the whole jungle rumbled when he roared. But Sabre wasn't actually like other lions at all. He wasn't fierce and scary – he was a cowardly lion. When other animals challenged him to a fight, he simply fiddled with his tail and looked silly. Even the dogs from the nearby village laughed at him.

Poor old Sabre felt very lonely.

Then one day, as Sabre was walking through the jungle, a terrible thing happened. Something flickered in the undergrowth and then flames began to leap out of the trees. A herd of elephants charged past, heading for the safety of the watering hole. More and more animals joined the stampede. Only Sabre and one of the dogs from the village stayed where they were.

"Help," barked the dog. "My puppy is back there in the fire."

Sabre didn't wait to hear more. He gave a great ROAR and leaped into the flames. Moments later, he was back holding a small black bundle in his gentle jaws. He dropped the puppy beside its mother and raced down to the waterhole. But he didn't stay long. He gulped down a mouthful of water and rushed back to the flames.

All the other animals watched in amazement as Sabre spat the water into the fire. What was he doing?

Suddenly, the elephants realised what he was trying to do. Sabre was trying to put out the fire. He was trying to save the jungle!

One by one, the elephants joined in, using their trunks to squirt water at the flames. Before long, the fire was out. Thanks to Sabre, the puppy and the jungle had been saved.

At long last, the other animals realised that Sabre wasn't a cowardly lion after all. He was a very brave lion. A very brave lion, who just didn't like fighting!

My Pigeon House

My pigeon house I open wide,
To set my pigeons free.
They fly around and up and down,
And land in the tallest tree.
And when they return from their merry flight,
They close their eyes and say good night.
Coo-coo-coo! Good night!

Cock-a-doodle-doo!

Cock-a-doodle-doo!
My dame has lost her shoe;
My master's lost his fiddling-stick,
And doesn't know what to do.

Cock-a-doodle-doo!
What is my dame to do?
Till master finds his fiddling-stick,
She'll dance without her shoe.

Cock-a-doodle-doo!
My dame has found her shoe,
And master's found his fiddling-stick;
Sing cock-a-doodle-doo!

The Cuckoo

Cuckoo, cuckoo,
What do you do?
"In April
I open my bill;
In May
I sing night and day;
In June
I change my tune;
In July
Away I fly;
In August
Away I must."

I Saw a Peacock

I saw a peacock with a fiery tail,
I saw a comet drop down hail,
I saw a cloud wrapped with ivy round,
I saw an oak tree upon the ground,
I saw a snail swallow a whale,
I saw the sea brimful of ale,
I saw a glass full fifteen feet deep,
I saw a well full of men that weep,
I saw red eyes of flaming fire,
I saw a house taller than the moon and higher,
I saw the sun at twelve midnight,
I saw the man that saw this wondrous sight.

Little Dragon

Little Dragon was reading a book all about a nasty man in a tin suit who bashes up poor little dragons. Little Dragon felt all worried and wobbly. Just then, Little Dragon heard voices.

"Oh, no!" thought Little Dragon. "Dragon-bashers!" And he hid under his blanket.

Outside, Princess Pippa, Prince Pip and Little Baron Boris were walking up the hill. Boris was making a lot of noise and waving a toy sword.

"Let's go on a dragon hunt," said Boris. "Are you coming?"

"No, thank you," said Pippa and Pip.

"Scaredy cats, scaredy cats!" sang Boris.

"We are not scaredy cats!" said Pip angrily.

"Look!" cried Boris. "Dragon footprints!"

They followed the footprints right up to Little Dragon's door.

"Er... you two go first," said Boris. "I'll stand outside and guard the door in case the dragon tries to escape."

Pip and Pippa pushed the door open. It was very dark and spooky inside the cave. They saw a light, and a big shadow that looked like... a dragon! They were very frightened!

"Who's there?" asked Pip bravely.

"It's me!" said Little Dragon.

"Are you a dragon?" asked Pippa.

"Yes," said Little Dragon.

"You're very small," said Pippa.

"I'm big on the inside," said Little Dragon, standing on tippy toes. Then he started to cry. "Are you going to bash me up now, like in my book?" he sniffed.

"Of course not," said Pippa, and she gave him a big hug.

"Let's just be friends," said Prince Pip. So that was settled.

"Would you like a snack?" asked Little Dragon.

"Oh, yes, please!" said Pippa and Pip. Little Dragon fetched a plate of jam doughnuts.

"Does your noisy friend with the pointy stick want one?" asked Little Dragon.

"Oh, you mean Boris," said Pippa. "I'm sure he'd like one. He's always hungry!"

"Would you like a doughnut, Boris?" asked Little Dragon.

"It's a dragon!" cried Little Baron Boris.

"Now who's a scaredy cat?" laughed Pip.

Soon it was time for Pip and Pippa to go.

"Can we be friends tomorrow?" asked Little Dragon.

"We'll be friends forever," said Pip and Pippa.

Chicken Licken

Chicken Licken was a little brown hen who lived on a farm with lots of other animals. Every day she sat under a big oak tree to take an afternoon nap. One day she was resting there when a big acorn fell down and landed with a loud bump on her head.

"Ouch!" said Chicken Licken, rubbing her head with her wing. **"The sky is falling!** I must tell the king. He will know what to do."

So Chicken Licken set off to see the king. On the way she met Cocky Locky.

"Where are you going?" he asked.

"I am going to see the king," replied Chicken Licken. **"The sky is falling!** He will know what to do."

"Then I will come with you," said Cocky Locky. So Chicken Licken and Cocky Locky ran on.

On the way, they met Ducky Lucky.

"Where are you going?" asked Ducky Lucky.

"We are going to see the king," said Chicken Licken. **"The sky is falling!** He will know what to do about it."

"Then I will come with you," said Ducky Lucky.

So Chicken Licken, Cocky Locky and Ducky Lucky ran on.

On the way, they met Goosey Loosey.

"Where are you going?" asked Goosey Loosey.

"We are going to see the king," said Chicken Licken. **"The sky is falling!** He will know what to do."

"Then I will come with you," said Goosey Loosey.

So Chicken Licken, Cocky Locky, Ducky Lucky and Goosey Loosey ran on.

On the way, they met Foxy Loxy, who was going for a stroll.

"Where are you going?" asked Foxy Loxy.

"We are going to see the king," said Chicken Licken. **"The sky is falling!** He will know what to do."

"Oh, dear," said Foxy Loxy, with a wicked glint in his eye, licking his lips. "I do believe you are going the wrong way."

"Goodness!" squawked Chicken Licken, getting in a flap. "Whatever shall we do? We must speak to the king as soon as possible."

"Then follow me!" said Foxy Loxy slyly. "I will show you the quickest way to go."

So Chicken Licken, Cocky Locky, Ducky Lucky and Goosey Loosey went on and on, following in Foxy Loxy's footsteps.

"Where are we going?" asked Chicken Licken. "Are we nearly there yet?"

Foxy Loxy smiled. "Just keep on following," he said.

Finally they arrived at a dark cave in the hillside.

"You must come in here!" said Foxy Loxy, leading the way into the cave. "This is a short cut. I am the only creature that knows about it. You will reach the king much more quickly if you come this way."

So Chicken Licken, Cocky Locky, Ducky Lucky and Goosey Loosey followed Foxy Loxy inside.

But oh, dearie me! It wasn't a short cut at all. It wasn't even a secret passageway. It was Foxy Loxy's den, and that crafty creature had dinner on his mind.

"I'm hungry!" he growled. "And now I am going to gobble you all up."

"Cock-a-doodle-do! Run for your lives!" cried Cocky Locky, as Foxy Loxy opened his jaws wide.

"Oh, no!" cried Chicken Licken, Ducky Lucky and Goosey Loosey, flapping their wings in alarm. "Run away! Run away!"

And that's exactly what those silly birds did – as fast as their legs would carry them. And they didn't stop running until they were home.

And as for Chicken Licken? She never did tell the king that the sky was falling down. Which is just as well, really.

A Silvery Trail

A silvery trail belongs to a snail,
Unless it's a slug... UGGH!

Arabella Miller

Little Arabella Miller found a hairy caterpillar.
First it crawled upon her mother,
Then upon her baby brother.
All said: "Arabella Miller, take away that caterpillar!"

Round and Round the Garden

Round and round the garden like a teddy bear.
One step, two step, tickle you under there.

Silly Sally

Silly Sally swiftly shooed seven silly sheep.
The seven silly sheep Silly Sally shooed shilly-shallied south.
These sheep shouldn't sleep in a shack;
Sheep should sleep in a shed.

Coo, Coo, What Shall I Do?

The dove says, "Coo, coo, what shall I do?
I can scarce maintain two."
"Pooh, pooh," says the wren; "I have got ten,
And keep them all like gentlemen!"

What Shall I Sing?

Sing, sing, what shall I sing?
The cat's run away with the pudding string!
Do, do, what shall I do?
The cat has bitten it quite in two!

Swan Swam Over the Sea

Swan swam over the sea,
Swim, swan, swim!
Swan swam back again,
Well swum, swan!

The Hare and the Tortoise

The hare was always boasting that he was the fastest runner in the world. Every time he saw the tortoise plodding slowly through the woods eating grass, he laughed at him.

"You really are the slowest creature I have ever seen," he said to the tortoise. "You have such short, stumpy little legs. It's no wonder it takes you all day to move from one tree to the next."

One day, the hare decided to challenge the other animals in the woods to a race.

"Will you race me?" he said to the fox. But the fox was too tired and volunteered to be the judge instead.

"Would you like to have a race?" the hare asked the squirrel. But the squirrel was too busy hiding nuts to be bothered with a race.

"I'll have a race with you," said a voice.

The hare looked around. There was no one there but the tortoise. "I beg your pardon?" said the hare.

"I will race you," said the tortoise.

The hare laughed until he thought his sides would split, but finally he agreed. So the hare and the tortoise lined up to race. Of course, the hare took off at top speed and was soon out of

sight, but the tortoise just followed, slowly and steadily.

After a while, the hare felt hot and thirsty, so he stopped at a stream for a drink. Meanwhile, the tortoise kept walking, without stopping for a moment.

The hare rejoined the race and set off at top speed again, but after a while he began to feel sleepy, so he decided to take a nap. The sun was going down by the time he woke up, but he was still sure he would beat the tortoise, and off he raced again.

At last, the finish line came into sight.

"They'll start cheering me any minute now," thought the hare, as he bounded across the line. But he was wrong. The crowds were already congratulating the tortoise.

"What happened to you, slowcoach?" teased the fox. "I thought you were the fastest animal in the world!"

Aesop's moral: Slow but steady wins the race.

All the Pretty Horses

Hush-a-bye, don't you cry,
Go to sleep, little baby.
And when you wake,
You shall have
All the pretty little horses.
Blacks and bays,
Dapple greys,
Coach and six white horses.
Hush-a-bye, don't you cry,
Go to sleep, little baby.

Five Little Owls

Five little owls in the old elm tree,
Fluffy and puffy as owls should be,
Blinking and winking with big round eyes
At the big round moon that hung in the skies.
As I passed by I heard one say,
"There'll be mouse for supper, there will today."
Then all of them hooted, "Tu-whit, tu-whoo!
Yes, mouse for supper, hoo hoo, hoo hoo."

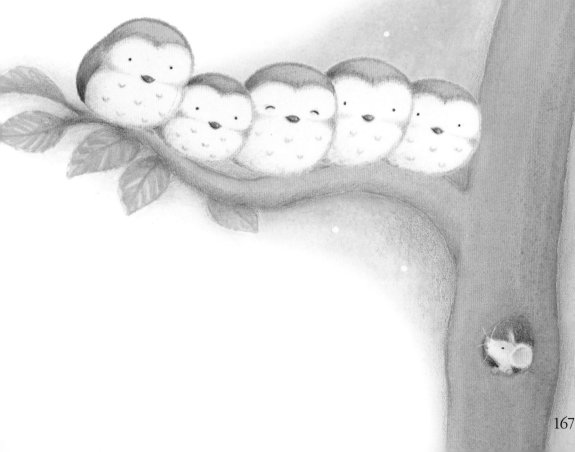

Little Red Riding Hood

Once upon a time a little girl lived with her mother on the edge of a forest. The little girl always wore a red cloak with a hood, so everyone called her Little Red Riding Hood.

One day, Little Red Riding Hood's mother asked her to take some food to her grandma on the other side of the forest. "Grandma isn't well," she explained. "So be sure to get there quickly and don't speak to any strangers along the way."

Little Red Riding hadn't gone very far when she met a wolf.

"Hello," purred the wolf. "Where are you going?"

"To see my sick grandma on the other side of the forest," replied Little Red Riding Hood, who had forgotten her mother's warning.

"Oh, really," said the wolf. And without saying another word, he dashed off.

The wolf didn't stop until he reached Grandma's house. He raced into her bedroom and gobbled her up. Then he put on her nightgown and climbed into her bed.

Soon Little Red Riding Hood arrived.

"Where are you, Grandma?" she called.

"I'm in bed," croaked the wolf.

"How strange she
sounds," thought Little
Red Riding Hood.
But when she entered
the bedroom she
gulped in surprise.

"What big eyes you have,
Grandma," she said.

"All the better to see you with," replied the wolf.

"What big ears you have," said Little Red Riding Hood.

"All the better to hear you with," said the wolf.

"What big teeth you have," spluttered the little girl.

"All the better to eat you with," roared the wolf, leaping up.

"Help!" screamed Little Red Riding Hood, as the wolf
gobbled her down in one gulp!

Her screams were so loud that a passing woodcutter rushed in
to see what was going on. When he saw the wolf's big belly,
he picked him up and shook him. The wolf gave a loud burp
and out shot Little Red Riding Hood, followed by Grandma.

They were rather rumpled and crumpled and very, very
annoyed. The wolf took one look at their angry faces, and the
woodcutter's axe, and raced away.

From that day on, the wolf never dared enter the forest, and
Little Red Riding Hood never spoke to strangers ever again.

The Vain Swan

Once upon a time four beautiful swans lived on a big river. The swans were the best of friends and were very happy. They looked so graceful and lovely that people always stopped to admire them. Then one day, something happened. Felix, the youngest swan, noticed his reflection for the first time. He was very pleased with what he saw and began to boast about how handsome he was.

"Look at my fine feathers," he said vainly. "I have the whitest feathers of any swan

on the river. I'm sure all the people come here to look at me. They're not interested in ordinary swans, like the rest of you."

At first the older swans tried to ignore him. But Felix kept staring at his reflection and remarking upon his beauty. Before too long, the other swans got fed up and decided to teach him a lesson.

"If people only come to see YOU," they honked, "then we don't need to stay here. We can find somewhere else fit for ordinary swans." And off they flew.

At first, Felix was so busy admiring his reflection that he

didn't really miss his friends. But, of course, it wasn't long before he started to feel very lonely. He hung his head and paddled sadly along the river.

The people who came down to the river couldn't help noticing that something was wrong. "Where have the other fine swans gone?" they asked. "There's only one sad-looking swan left."

After many days, Felix realised how silly he had been. He knew he had to do something, so he soared into the sky.

Over the countryside he flew, in search of his friends. At last he saw three beautiful swans swimming on a fine lake.

He swooped down shyly, afraid that they would send him away.

"I've missed you," he told them. "I'm sorry I was so vain and silly."

Of course, his friends didn't chase him away. They were delighted to see Felix. "We've missed you, too," they honked. "Why don't you stay with us ordinary swans?"

Felix was overjoyed. "I'd love to," he honked in reply, "but... there is nothing ordinary about you!"

What's the Weather?

When a cow tries to scratch her ear,
It means a shower is very near.
When she thumps her ribs with her tail,
Look out for thunder, lightning and hail.

The Frog

A little green frog once lived in a pool,
The sun was hot and the water cool.
He sat in the pool the whole day long,
And sang a dear little, queer little song.
"Jaggery do, quaggery dee,
No one was ever so happy as me."

To Market

To market, to market, to buy a fat pig,
Home again, home again, jiggety-jig.
To market, to market, to buy a fat hog,
Home again, home again, jiggety-jog.

Little Poll Parrot

Little Poll Parrot
Sat in the garret,
Eating toast and tea;
A little brown mouse,
Jumped into the house
And stole it away, you see.

B-I-N-G-O!

There was a farmer had a dog,
And Bingo was his name-O.
B-I-N-G-O!
B-I-N-G-O!
B-I-N-G-O!
And Bingo was his name-O!

Diddlety, Diddlety, Dumpty

Diddlety, diddlety, dumpty,
The cat ran up the plum tree;
Half a crown
To fetch her down,
Diddlety, diddlety, dumpty.

The Opossum's Tail

Once upon a time, the opossum had a long and bushy tail. He was so proud of it, he spent all his time washing and brushing it, and he was always boasting to the other animals that he had the finest tail in the whole forest.

One day, the rabbit decided to play a trick on the opossum and invited him to a dance. The opossum accepted at once. It would be a chance to show off his fabulous tail to all the animals in the area.

"Why don't I ask the cricket to come and groom your tail for you, so that it looks its best?" the rabbit suggested.

The opossum agreed, so the following day, the cricket arrived with a bag containing a comb and scissors, and a long piece of ribbon.

"It is a great honour for you to be allowed to groom my beautiful tail," the vain opossum told the cricket.

"Yes, it is something I will be proud to tell my grandchildren," the cricket agreed. "I have brought this ribbon to wrap around your tail when I have combed and trimmed it. That way, it won't get dirty on the way to the dance."

The opossum lay down and the cricket began work, gently grooming the long, bushy tail. It was so soothing that the opossum soon grew sleepy, and before long he was snoring.

When he woke up, his tail was neatly wrapped in the ribbon.

As the opossum arrived at the dance, the rabbit offered to undo the ribbon for him.

"Please do," agreed the opossum, eager to join all the other animals and show off his beautiful tail.

As soon as he stepped onto the dance floor, the opossum looked around. All the other animals were pointing at his tail.

"Yes, it is very fine," he smiled vainly – until he heard the sound of laughter above the music. They were not admiring his tail at all – **they were making fun of it!**

The opossum looked down and gasped. The cricket had cut off every single hair, and his bushy tail was now as bald and scaly as a lizard's.

He was so embarrassed that he didn't know what to do – so he rolled over on his back to hide his ugly, bald tail. And to this day, the opossum's tail is bare – and if he is surprised or embarrassed, he will roll over onto his back.

Little Mouse

I have seen you, little mouse,
Running all about the house,
Through the hole your little eye
In the darkness, peeping sly,
Hoping soon some crumbs to steal,
To make quite a hearty meal.
Look before you venture out,
See if kitty is about.
If she's gone, you'll quickly run
To the pantry for some fun;
Round about the dishes creep,
Taking into each a peep,
To choose the daintiest that's there,
Eating crumbs without a care.

Sing a Song of Sixpence

Sing a song of sixpence,
A pocket full of rye.
Four and twenty blackbirds,
Baked in a pie.

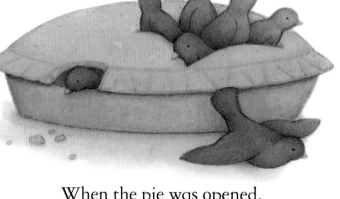

When the pie was opened,
The birds began to sing;
Wasn't that a dainty dish,
To set before the king?
The king was in his counting house,
Counting out his money;
The queen was in the parlour,
Eating bread and honey.
The maid was in the garden,
Hanging out the clothes;
When down came a blackbird
And pecked off her nose!

Dreamtime

What do creatures dream of
When they close their eyes?
Do they dream like you and I
Beneath the starry skies?
Do donkeys dream of pulling carts,
And munching bales of hay?

Do piglets dream of muck and mud,
And all the games they play?
Do buttercups and fresh green grass
Fill a cow's sweet dreams,
When they fall asleep at night
Beneath the moonlit beams?

And how do sheep fall asleep?
By counting dogs and cats?
Do kittens dream of bowls of cream,
And chasing mice and rats?

Do roosters dream of morning time,
And crowing very loud?
Or do they dream of bossing hens,
And strutting, oh, so proud?
What do creatures dream of
When they close their eyes?
Do they dream like you and I
Beneath the moonlit skies?

Alice and the White Rabbit

One day, Alice was sitting beside a river with her sister, when something curious happened. A white Rabbit with pink eyes ran past.

"Oh, dear! Oh, dear! I shall be too late," he said. Then he took a watch out of his vest pocket and hurried on.

Alice quickly leaped to her feet and followed the Rabbit down a large rabbit hole. The rabbit hole went straight on like a tunnel for some way, and then dipped so suddenly that Alice didn't have time to stop herself. She found herself falling **down...**

"I must be getting near the centre of the Earth," Alice thought to herself. **Down, down, down** Alice kept falling.

Suddenly she landed in a heap at the bottom. When she got up she found herself in a long hall, lined with doors. At the end was a little three-legged glass table. There was nothing on it but a tiny golden key. Alice tried the key in all the doors, but it wouldn't open any of them. Then she noticed a low curtain she had not seen before. Behind it was a tiny door.

She turned the key in the lock and it opened. The door led into a beautiful garden, but Alice could not even get her head through the doorway. She went back to the table and saw a little bottle labelled **"DRINK ME!"**

Once she was sure it wasn't poison, Alice drank it and shrank. But when she went back to the door, she remembered that she had left the key on the table. Alice didn't know what to do. Then she saw a cake marked **"EAT ME!"**

Alice ate it and began to grow. Soon she was so large her head touched the ceiling!

Alice began to cry, and was soon surrounded by a large pool of tears. She was wondering what to do, when who should come along but the white Rabbit. He was carrying a pair of white gloves and a large fan.

"If you please, sir…" began Alice.

The Rabbit dropped the gloves and fan, and scurried away.

"How strange everything is today," said Alice, picking up the gloves and the fan. "I'm not myself at all." Then she began fanning herself as she wondered who she might be instead.

After a while, Alice looked down at her hands. She was surprised to see that she had put on one of the Rabbit's little white gloves.

"I must be growing smaller again," she thought.

Alice realised that it was the fan that was making her shrink, so she dropped it quickly and ran to the door. Suddenly, she remembered that the key was still on the table.

"Drat," she said. "Things can't possibly get any worse." But she was wrong. SPLASH! She fell into her sea of tears.

"I wish I hadn't cried so much!" wailed Alice.

Just then, she heard something splashing. It was a Mouse.

"Mouse, do you know the way out of this pool?" asked Alice. The Mouse didn't reply.

"Perhaps he speaks French," thought Alice. So she began again. "Où est mon chat?" which was the first sentence in her French book and meant "Where is my cat?"

The Mouse leaped out of the water in fright.

"I'm sorry!" cried Alice. "I didn't mean to scare you."

"Come ashore," said the Mouse. "I'll tell you why cats frighten me."

By this time the pool was crowded with birds and animals. There was a Duck, a Dodo, a Parrot, an Eaglet and other curious creatures, too. Together, they all swam to the shore.

The birds and animals were dripping wet.

"Let's have a race," said the Dodo. "It will help us to dry off." And he began to mark out a course.

Then, when everyone was dotted along the course, they began starting and stopping whenever they felt like it. It was impossible to tell when the race was over, but after half an hour, they were all very dry.

"But who won the race?" asked the Mouse.

"Everyone," said the Dodo. "Alice will give out prizes." So Alice handed round some sweets she had in her pocket.

"But she must have a prize, too," said the Mouse.

"What else have you got in your pocket?" asked the Dodo.

Alice handed over a thimble, and he gave it back to her saying, "I beg you to accept this thimble."

Alice accepted as solemnly as she could, and then they all sat down to hear the Mouse's tale. But Alice was so tired, she just couldn't concentrate, and the Mouse stomped away in a huff!

"I wish my cat, Dinah, were here," said Alice. "She'd soon fetch him back."

Then she tried to tell everyone about Dinah – but they were scared of cats too, and ran away. Poor Alice was alone again.

Pitty, Patty, Polt

Pitty, patty, polt,
Shoe the wild colt;
Here a nail, there a nail,
Pitty, patty, polt.

Higglety, Pigglety, Pop!

Higglety, pigglety, pop!
The dog has eaten the mop;
The pig's in a hurry, the cat's in a flurry,
Higglety, pigglety, pop!

Where Has My Little Dog Gone?

Where, oh where
Has my little dog gone?
Oh where, oh where can he be?
With his ears cut short,
And his tail cut long,
Oh where, oh where can he be?

A Duck and a Drake

A duck and a drake,
And a nice barley cake,
With a penny to pay the old baker;
Hippety hop, we're off to the shop,
If she won't come, we'll take her.

Thirty White Horses

Thirty white horses upon a red hill.
Now they tramp, now they champ,
Now they stand still.

A Cat Came Fiddling

A cat came fiddling out of a barn,
With a pair of bagpipes under her arm.
She could sing nothing but fiddle dee dee,
The mouse has married the bumble bee.
Pipe, cat! Dance, mouse!
We'll have a wedding at our good house.

Rama Has Toothache

Rama the tiger was usually very friendly, but one morning she awoke with a loud roar – and she didn't stop roaring all day. Whenever anyone passed her cave, she roared. If anyone asked her what was wrong, she roared. Soon everyone in the jungle was creeping around on tiptoe. Everyone was much too afraid to go near her. Everyone, that is, but Bat.

"What is the matter?" he asked.

"Buzz off!" roared Rama.

Bat shook his head. "I'm not going until you tell me."

"I've got a toothache!" growled Rama angrily.

"Then we will have to pull out your bad tooth," replied her friend.

"Oh, no, you don't," roared Rama. And to make sure that no one touched her tooth, she stuck her head out of her cave and roared so loudly that the jungle shook. "If anyone touches me, I'll bite them," she cried. And just to prove it, she bit a nearby tree.

As she bit, Rama felt something in her mouth move. Her sore tooth had come out in the tree trunk!

"Hooray!" cried Rama happily. "My toothache is gone."

But no one was happier than her friends!

Nine Bored Wolves

Nine bored wolves stand around and wait,
One goes hunting, then there are eight.
Eight bored wolves decide to do some tricks,
Two play 'Chase my Tail', then there are six.
Six bored wolves – they wouldn't hurt a flea,
Three find a trail to sniff, then there are three.
Three bored wolves decide to have some fun,
So they all play Wolf Chase... and then there are none.

Don't Be Scared!

"Little Cub," said Dad, "I think the time's right
for you to come out with me to explore tonight."

Little Cub peered at the evening sky. The sun was slipping
down behind the trees. Shadows stretched across the plain.
As they set off, Little Cub shivered, and suddenly stopped.

"What's that high up there in that tree?"
he asked. "Two great big eyes watching me."

"Look closer, Little Cub. That thing up there
is just old Owl. Did he give you a scare?" asked Dad.

"Dad," smiled Little Cub, "Owl won't give me a scare.
He can't do that, as long as you're there."

Suddenly, Little Cub stopped. "What's that black shape

hanging down from that tree?
I felt it reaching out for me."

"Look closer, Little Cub.
That thing up there
is just old Snake. Did he give
you a scare?" asked Dad.

"Dad," smiled Little Cub,
"Snake won't give me a scare.
He can't do that, as long as
you're there."

Suddenly, Little Cub stopped.
"What's that I can hear
behind that tree?

There's a huge black shadow following me."

"Look closer, Little Cub. That thing back there is just old Elephant. Did he give you a scare?" asked Dad.

"Dad," smiled Little Cub, "Elephant won't give me a scare. He can't do that, as long as you're there."

Dad and Little Cub walked on. Suddenly, Dad stopped.

"What's that?" he asked.

"Toowhit, toowhoo! Ssss, ssss! Terummmp, terummmp!"

The animals jumped out at Dad. Dad jumped!

"Don't be scared," laughed Little Cub.

"Sorry, Lion! Did we give you a scare?" asked the animals, laughing.

"No!" said Dad. "You couldn't give me a scare. Not as long as Little Cub is there."

Then, side by side, Little Cub and Dad headed for home.

Doctor Finley Pig

Finley was a very happy pig.
Life just couldn't be better.
"It's alright for you!"
said Agatha Chicken,
who was always sticking
her beak in other people's
business. "This is a busy farm,
lazybones," she clucked.

"But I'm not a lazybones," replied the happy little porker.
"I'm Finley."

"Don't be cheeky!" Agatha flapped her wings and squawked
until Finley ran away.

Finley sat under a tree to think. Taking mud baths was
a lovely way to spend your time, but he did want to be a big
help on the busy farm, too. What would he be good at?

Mummy Pig was puzzled. "Where are you going with all
those things, Finley?" she asked.

"I'm not Finley, I'm Doctor Pig!"
replied Finley. "And I'm
late for my first patient.
What seems to be the
trouble, Mrs Moo?"

Mrs Moo mooed.
"Don't say moo, say
ahhh!" said Finley.

"Finley, there's nothing wrong with my leg," said Mrs Moo, as Finley tried to tie a bandage around it.

"Hold still for Doctor Pig, please!" said Finley.

Chester Sheep was not good at having his heart listened to – he wouldn't stop munching.

The geese, Heidi and Dora, refused their medicine.

And Tilly the sheepdog? Well, she just ran away...

Being a doctor was really hard work, but the most difficult patients of all were the chickens. There were just so many of them, and they all wanted to be first in the queue.

At the end of a long day, Mummy Pig was pleased to see Finley.

"I'm very good at being a doctor," said Finley. "But I'm even better at being me."

Life just couldn't be better!

Mabel Gets Lost

One sunny day, Mrs Duck took her ducklings for a swim.

"Whatever you do, stay close, and don't wander off," she warned her brood.

But Mabel, the smallest duckling, wasn't listening. She was too busy chasing butterflies. Mabel waddled along behind a colourful butterfly until it disappeared across the river. Then she looked around. She  had wandered a long way from home, and had never seen this part of the river before. But Mabel didn't mind. There were lots of interesting things to see. She watched a blue kingfisher diving for fish. Then she saw some otters playing on the bank. Above, a flock of swans soared across the sky.

"Quack, quack!" she cried. "This is an exciting place!"

She called out to the otters, but they were too busy messing around to hear her. Suddenly, Mabel began to miss her mum and her brothers and sisters.

"I'd better go home," she quacked. But when she looked around, Mabel didn't know which way to go.

"Oh, no," she wailed. "I'm lost." And she sat down beside

the river to cry. She had been crying for a few minutes when the water in front her began to ripple. Then two bulging eyes, followed by a green head, popped up. It was her friend Herbert the frog. Mabel gulped and tried to wipe away her tears.

"What's wrong?" Herbert asked kindly.

"I'm lost," wept Mabel. "And I miss my mum."

"Don't worry," croaked Herbert. "Jump into the river and swim behind me. I'll show you the way home."

So Mabel followed Herbert downstream until they bumped into Mrs Duck and the other ducklings.

"Hooray! I'm home at last!" quacked Mabel, leaping out of the water and rushing to her mum's side.

Mrs Duck was so pleased to see her that she forgot to be angry.

"I'll stay close to you from now on," quacked Mabel.

Tia and Teddy

Tia Mouse's favourite toy was Teddy.

Teddy went with Tia everywhere. When Teddy was with Tia, Tia wasn't scared of anything. She wasn't scared of climbing to the top of the stalks of corn in the field nearby, or bigger mice, or doing somersaults, or anything at all.

"You and Teddy are so brave!" Mum would say, as Tia told her about another one of their adventures together.

One afternoon, though, Tia looked all through the mouse hole, but she couldn't find Teddy anywhere.

Tia started to cry. "Mum! Teddy's gone missing!"

Mum came out of the study. "I'm sure he's somewhere, Tia," she said. "Don't worry, we'll find him."

"I'm scared without Teddy," said Tia.

Tia and Mum went to look for Teddy. They looked in the corn field. Then they looked down by the stream. And there was Teddy! He was propped up against a tree.

"We were looking at the fish this morning with Dad," said Tia. "Teddy must have decided to watch them for a bit longer."

"Well he's found now," said Mum, giving them both a big hug.

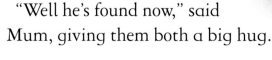

That night Tia couldn't sleep. She
lay awake and looked at the
dark. Suddenly she felt
scared of the shadows.
She crept out of bed
and went into her
mum's room.

"I'm scared, Mum,"
said Tia.

"But you're never
scared when you're
with Teddy," said Mum.

"But what if I lose him
again?" said Tia.

Mum smiled. "Let me tell you
a secret," she said. " Do you know what Teddy said to me
when we came back from the stream this morning? He told me
that he was scared when he was on his own by the stream, but
he's never scared when he's with you, because you're so brave."

"So I think Teddy's the brave one," said Tia...

"... but he thinks you are!" finished Mum.

"Perhaps we're both brave," said Tia. "Do you know, I think
I might be ready to go back to bed now." She gave Mum a big
hug, and Mum hugged her and Teddy back.

"Night, night, Tia. Night, night, Teddy," said Mum.

"Night, night, Mum," said Tia. "Teddy says 'night night' as
well. And he says to tell you he's not scared any more."

Naja Keeps Cool

It was a scorching hot day, and Naja the Cobra was so hot that she didn't know what to do with herself.

"I'll have to find ssssomewhere cool to sleep," she hissed. She looked around and saw a big rock. "I can find sssshade under that," she thought. But as soon as she touched the rock she spat out an angry hiss. It had been in the sun for so long that it was burning hot.

Naja slithered over to a pile of leaves. "I'll hide beneath these," she thought. But when she tried to crawl under she was chased out by an army of angry ants.

By now Naja was so hot and sleepy that she could barely move. Then she saw the house...

Slowly, she slithered through the open door – but quickly raced back out again with an angry woman on her tail.

"Get out," yelled the woman, thumping Naja with a broom. Naja slithered away, down the steps, and into the cellar.

"**Ahh!**" she sighed. "This is lovely." Then she spotted a cool water pitcher. Slithering over, she wrapped herself around the pitcher.

"**Wonderful!**" hissed Naja happily. At last she could sleep in peace.

What's in a Name?

One morning, Tailorbird was busy flittering around the forest when a curious little mongoose wandered along.

The mongoose watched the busy bird gathering things, and then coughed to get her attention. "Excuse me? Why are you called Tailorbird?" he asked. "If you ask me, you should be called Busy bird."

"**Cheeup! Cheeup!**" chirped Tailorbird. "Sorry, I'm too busy to talk right now. You'll just have to wait and see."

So the mongoose sat down to watch. First Tailorbird used her sharp beak to pierce tiny holes in two big leaves. Then she threaded a long piece of spider's silk through the holes to join the leaves together. Next she lined the cradle of leaves with soft wool to make it warm and cosy. When she was finished, she poked her head out of her cosy new nest.

"Do you still wonder why I'm called Tailorbird?" she chirped.

Mongoose smiled and shook his head. "No!" he laughed. "The answer is plain to see! It's because you are so good at sewing, just like a tailor who makes clothes!"

Little Duckling

Little duckling, can you spare
Some feathers for my bed,
To make my pillow soft and warm,
So I may rest my head?

A Little Pig

A little pig found a fifty-dollar note,
And purchased a hat and a very fine coat,
With cravat, shirt collar and gold-headed cane,
Then proud as could be, did he march up the lane.

A Frisky Lamb

A frisky lamb,
And a frisky child,
Playing their pranks
In a cowslip meadow:
The sky all blue,
And the air all mild,
And the fields all sun
And the lanes half shadow.

Bat, Bat

Bat, bat,
Come under my hat,
And I'll give you a slice of bacon;
And when I bake,
I'll give you a cake,
If I am not mistaken.

Hungry Tiger

Hungry tiger in a tree,
Watching you,
Watching me.
You best take care,
My little friend,
Unless you want a sticky end!

Dolphin Song

The day is grey, but the dolphins play,
They dance and leap and sing.
They dive through the waves,
And they're ever so brave!
A dolphin's a wonderful thing.

Mars the Pony

Once upon a time there was a pony called Mars. He lived at a riding school with lots of other ponies. Mars was too young to be ridden, so he stayed in the field all day while all the other ponies taught little boys and girls to ride. Mars was very happy. He loved munching on grass. He loved jumping the fences put up for the bigger horses to jump. But best of all he loved being groomed and cuddled by all the boys and girls.

Mars was very happy with his life until, one day, one of the grooms put a bridle on him.

"It's time for your training to begin," she whispered, rubbing him kindly on the nose. "Soon you will be ridden like all the other ponies."

"Oh, goody!" thought Mars. "Being ridden looks easy. I'm sure I'll be really good at it."

But Mars couldn't have been more wrong. Being ridden wasn't at all easy. And he wasn't very good at it. In fact, having a person on your back was rather scary. It made him feel all wobbly and unbalanced. And the world outside his field was full of terrifying things, like noisy tractors, screaming children and, worst of all, plastic bags that flapped in the wind.

Mars really wished that he didn't have to be ridden. He wished that everyone would just leave him alone in his field. So one night, he came up with a plan. He wouldn't let anyone ride him. The following morning, when one of the grooms tried to catch him, he put back his ears, kicked up his hooves and raced away. After that he tried to kick or bite anyone who came near him. Soon no one dared approach him and Mars was left well alone. At first, Mars was very pleased with himself. But soon he began to feel rather lonely. He didn't know what to do. He didn't want to be ridden but he did miss being groomed and cuddled.

Then one night, as Mars was dozing in his field, something magical happened. A dazzling white horse appeared before him.

"Don't be afraid," whispered the horse. "I am your guardian angel. I have come to help you. Follow me!"

In an instant, the white horse whirled around and soared into the sky. Mars galloped after him. They galloped across the night sky until they came to a field.

"Look down," said the white horse kindly.

Mars looked down and saw a small pony leaping easily over a jump with a little girl on his back. Mars blinked and neighed with amazement. That pony was him. But who was that girl who was riding on his back?

"That's Katy," said the white horse gently, as if reading his thoughts. "See how gentle and kind she is. She would never hurt you."

Mars stared and stared until everything turned into a misty blur before his eyes. Then he suddenly blinked and found himself back in his own field at the riding stables. The white

horse had vanished and he was alone once more.

"Oh," sighed Mars sadly. "It must have been a dream."

He couldn't stop thinking about the kind little girl he had seen.

The following morning, Mars was hiding in the corner of his field when a little girl came to the gate.

"Hello Mars," she called, waving a carrot in his direction. Mars crept out from his hiding place and stared. It was the girl from the dream. It was Katy!

Katy climbed the gate and walked slowly towards Mars, taking care not to frighten him.

"Come on, boy," she whispered softly. "I won't hurt you." Then she stood still and waited.

At first, Mars refused to budge. Then his curiosity got the better of him and he crept slowly towards her. Still she didn't move. Suddenly, Mars felt quite brave. He walked slowly up to Katy's shoulder and lowered his head. Katy put out her hand and stroked his head. Then she gave him the carrot. As Mars crunched the carrot, Katy gently put a head collar over his head.

"There you go, boy," she said softly.

After that, Mars always allowed Katy to catch him. And soon he even let her sit on his back. By the end of the summer he and Katy were the very best of friends and sailing over jumps together. And when the stables held their summer show, guess who won the jumping competition? Mars, of course.

Thanks to the mysterious white horse, Mars had allowed himself to trust again.

Anna Maria

Anna Maria, she sat on the fire;
The fire was too hot, she sat on the pot;
The pot was too round, she sat on the ground;
The ground was too flat, she sat on the cat;
The cat ran away with Maria on her back.

Come Dance a Jig

Come dance a jig
With my granny's pig,
With a raudy, rowdy, dowdy;
Come dance a jig
With my granny's pig,
And we shall all sing loudly.

Froggy

Froggy did a courting go,
"Heigh ho!" said Froggy.
Froggy did a courting go,
Even though his mother said, "No!"
With a rowley, powley, fiddle dee dee,
"Heigh ho!" says Froggy.

First in a Carriage

First in a carriage,
Second in a gig,
Third on a donkey,
And fourth on a pig.

For Want of a Nail

For want of a nail the shoe was lost,
For want of a shoe the horse was lost,
For want of a horse the rider was lost,
For want of a rider the battle was lost,
For want of a battle the kingdom was lost,
And all for the want of a horseshoe nail.

Dear Little Friend

Dear little friend, O la!
I heard a lambkin cry, "Baa!"
I said, "So you have lost Mamma? Ah!"
The little lamb, as I said so,
Frisking about the fields did go,
And, frisking, trod upon my toe. Oh!

The Mouse and the Weasel

One day, a hungry mouse came across a basket of corn in a barn. There was a lid on the basket, and the farmer had put a brick on top to keep out mice and rats, but the little mouse was starving and determined to get to the corn.

The mouse ran **round** and **round** and up and down the basket until he found a narrow space between the strips of wood. Normally the mouse would never have been able to squeeze through such a tiny hole, but he was so thin by now that he just managed to wriggle his way into the basket.

The mouse was so hungry that he ate, and ate, and ate. And then he ate some more. At last he felt satisfied and burrowed his way back through the corn, until he found the space in the basket again.

But the hole suddenly looked very, very small – and the mouse was feeling very, very fat! In fact, his stomach was three times as big it had been when he had squeezed his way in.

The mouse pushed his head through the hole and wriggled. It was no use. He couldn't get through. So he tried to pull his head back in again, only to find that he was completely stuck. He couldn't move backwards or forwards.

Just then, a weasel passed by. He saw the mouse's head sticking out of the basket and guessed what had happened.

"I know what you've been doing," laughed Weasel. "You've been stuffing yourself with food and now you are stuck. It's your own fault. I don't have any sympathy for you, I'm afraid! You will just have to wait there without eating until you are thin enough to get out again."

And that's exactly what the greedy little mouse had to do.

Aesop's moral: Greed often leads to misfortune.

Curious Kitten

Snowball was a very curious kitten. One day, she watched Mrs Duck lead her ducklings across the yard. They looked so funny waddling along that Snowball decided to join them.

"I wonder what it's like being a duck," she thought. She scurried along behind the ducklings, trying her best to quack – but all she could manage was a strange "Meeaak!"

Snowball watched as the ducklings nibbled the grass on the riverbank. She tried a little herself, but it made her cough. Then she watched as the ducklings followed their mother into the water.

"Swimming looks easy," she thought, so she jumped in. SPLASH! Of course, Snowball quickly discovered that swimming wasn't easy for a kitten at all.

"Help!" she spluttered, as she tried to keep her head above water.

Luckily, Tank the sheepdog was nearby. He leaped in and pulled her out before she could come to any harm.

Once Snowball had recovered, she crept back into the house and lay in front of the warm fire.

"I'd far rather be a kitten than a duck," she purred.

Shy Octopus

Harry was a shy octopus who lived in a quiet corner of the coral reef. He rarely came out and if he bumped into anyone, he would squeeze himself into the nearest crack and hide – because, being a rubbery octopus, he could squeeze himself into places that no one else could reach.

One day, Harry was hiding when he heard a shout.

"Help!" cried a tiny voice. "It's me, Crab! I've fallen down a crack and I can't get out."

Harry peered out of his hidey-hole and watched as the other sea creatures did their best to rescue their friend.

First Seahorse tried to squeeze into the crack… then Angelfish… and finally Eel. But it was no use. They were all far too big. Harry knew that he would have to help, so he coughed shyly.

"Allow me," he said. And much to everyone's surprise, he squeezed his rubbery body into the crack and used a long tentacle to pull the tiny crab free. Everyone cheered.

"My hero!" sighed the tiny crab, smiling at Harry.

Harry blushed but felt very pleased. Maybe making friends wasn't going to be so difficult after all.

Kiera the Kite

It was a dark and stormy night, and Kiera the kite was one
of the few creatures who dared to go out. She had a chick
to feed and had left her mountaintop nest to hunt.

At last Kiera managed to snare a juicy mouse and set off for
home. She flapped her powerful wings and battled against the
wind. The wind was so strong that she couldn't fly very fast.
It was almost dawn when she finally spotted her nest. She
swooped down in triumph, and then shuddered to a halt.

"Squawk!" she cried. Her nest was empty! Where was her
baby? Kiera hopped around in alarm.
She didn't know what to do. Then
she had an idea. She flapped her
wings and soared
high into the sky. Hovering
above the ground, she
scanned the area with
sharp eyes. Almost
immediately she spotted
a movement far below
and swooped down. Kiera
screeched with joy. There was her
little chick, sitting safely on a rocky ledge.

"I'm okay," squeaked the little chick. "I jumped out of the
nest because it was swaying in the wind."

"I think it's time to teach you how to fly," smiled Kiera.

A New Pool for Otter

Otter had lived in the animal sanctuary for as long as he could remember. Then, one day, his keeper lifted him out of his pen and placed him in a crate. Otter was so scared that he couldn't move. He curled into a ball and shook with fright as the lid closed and everything went dark.

"What's happening?" he wondered.

Otter felt himself being carried along and put down. Then a door slammed, and an engine roared into life. The engine purred as Otter bumped gently around in his crate. Finally the engine stopped and the door was opened.

Otter's crate was lifted out and placed on to the ground. Sunlight flooded in as the lid opened. Otter blinked and sniffed the air. He looked around before creeping out. Suddenly, he was bursting with happiness. There in front of him was a woodland pool, twinkling in the sun.

"Welcome home!" smiled his keeper.

SPLASH! Otter dived into the crystal-clear water and darted after the fish. He was free…

Rikki-Tikki-Tavi

Rikki-Tikki-Tavi was a small furry mongoose. He looked like a little cat with his fur and his tail, but his head and the way he acted were more like a weasel. He could fluff up his tail until it looked like a bottle brush, and his war cry, as he scuttled through the long grass, was **"Rikk-tikk-tikki-tchk!"**

Rikki-Tikki lived a happy life with his parents in the jungle. Then one day, a great flood washed him from his burrow. When he revived, he was lying in the sun on a path in front of a bungalow.

"Look, Mum!" said a young boy. "A dead mongoose."

"No, he's not dead," replied the boy's mother. "Let's take him in to dry. The poor thing is exhausted."

The little boy was called Teddy, and he lived in the bungalow with his parents. The family was so kind that Rikki-Tikki decided to stay.

One morning, Rikki-Tikki decided to explore the yard.

He hadn't gone far when he heard somebody crying. It was Darzee, the tailorbird, and his wife.

"What's the matter?" asked Rikki-Tikki.

"Nag has eaten one of our babies," sobbed Darzee.

"Oh, dear," said Rikki-Tikki. "But who's Nag?"

Before Darzee could answer, there was a hiss, and a black cobra slithered by. He was five feet long from tongue to tail.

"I am Nag," hissed the beast. "Be afraid. Be very afraid."

For a moment Rikki-Tikki felt the tiniest bit afraid, but he knew that it was every brave mongoose's duty to fight deadly snakes. So he held his tail high and puffed out his cheeks. He looked terrifying! Nag began to shake, until he saw the grass rustle behind Rikki-Tikki and knew that help was at hand. He tried to distract the little mongoose.

"Hey!" he hissed. "You eat eggs. Why should I not eat birds?"

"Watch out behind you!" cried Darzee.

Rikki-Tikki leaped up into the air and just missed being struck by Nagaina, Nag's wicked wife. Rikki-Tikki landed on her back and bit, before jumping clear of the wriggling beast.

Rikki-Tikki's eyes glowed red with rage as Nag and Nagaina disappeared into the grass.

Teddy came running down the path to pat Rikki-Tikki.

"Our mongoose has saved

us from a snake!" he cried.

That night, Teddy carried him off to bed and insisted that Rikki-Tikki sleep under his chin. But as soon as Teddy was asleep, Rikki-Tikki went exploring.

The house was quiet, but when Rikki-Tikki went into the bathroom he heard Nag and Nagaina whispering outside.

"When all the people are gone," hissed Nagaina, "Rikki-Tikki will have to leave. Then we will be the king and queen of the yard. Remember, bite the big man first."

Rikki-Tikki shook with rage at hearing this, but he hid as the giant cobra slithered into the bathroom. Then he waited until Nag had fallen asleep, and sank his fangs into the cobra's head. He held on tight as Nag thrashed around. Suddenly a gun went off, and Nag was no more. Teddy's father had heard the noise and had shot the wicked snake.

The following morning, Rikki-Tikki set out to deal with Nagaina himself.

"Where is Nagaina?" he asked Darzee.

"On the rubbish heap," he replied.

"Do you know where she keeps her eggs?" asked Rikki-Tikki.

"In the melon bed," replied Darzee. "Are you going to eat them?"

"Not exactly," replied the mongoose. "If your wife can keep Nagaina busy, you'll soon see what I have in mind."

So Darzee's wife left her husband to

guard the nest and fluttered over to Nagaina.

When the wicked cobra saw the little bird, she slithered after her. As soon as the coast was clear, Rikki-Tikki rushed to the cobra's nest and began to smash the eggs.

Suddenly Darzee's wife screamed.

"Nagaina is up at the house."

Rikki-Tikki scuttled to the house as fast as he could. Nagaina was about to strike at Teddy!

"Look!" taunted Rikki-Tikki, holding up Nagaina's last egg in front of the evil snake.

"If you give me that I will go away forever," cried Nagaina. But Rikki-Tikki knew she was lying. Nagaina struck out, and Rikki-Tikki leaped out of the way. Again and again the snake struck. Each time Rikki-Tikki danced out of the way.

Suddenly Nagaina grabbed the egg in her mouth and flew like an arrow down the path. Rikki-Tikki bit the end of her tail, and the two creatures disappeared down a hole.

Just when his friends feared the worst, Rikki-Tikki popped out. "It's over," he said.

And that's the last time a cobra ever dared set foot inside the walls of Rikki-Tikki's garden.

The Nesting Hour

Feathered friend has gone to bed,
Little wing to hide his head.
Mother birds must slumber too,
Just like baby chicks do.
When the stars begin to rise,
Birds and babies close their eyes.

Robert Barnes

Robert Barnes, fellow fine,
Can you shoe this horse of mine?
Yes, good sir, that I can,
As well as any other man.
There's a nail, and there's a prod,
And now, good sir, your horse is shod.

Whisky, Frisky

Whisky, frisky, hippity, hop,
Up he climbs to the treetop.
Whirly, twirly, round and round,
Down he scampers to the ground.
Where's his supper?
In a shell…
Snappy, cracky, out it fell.

Three Cows

There was an old woman who had three cows,
Rosy and Colin and Dun.
Rosy and Colin were sold at the fair,
And Dun broke her heart in a fit of despair,
So there was an end of her three cows,
Rosy and Colin and Dun.

The Little Black Dog

The little black dog ran round the house,
And set the bull a-roaring,
And drove the monkey in the boat,
Who set the oars a-rowing,
And scared the cock upon the rock,
Who cracked his throat with crowing.

There Was an Old Crow

There was an old crow
Sat upon a clod:
There's an end of my song,
That's odd!

Little Dragon's Wagon

Little Dragon was walking in the sunshine. Buzz! went the bees. Tweet! went the birds. Squeak! went the bush...

"What can that be?" wondered Little Dragon.

It was a pull-along wagon, with one broken wheel spinning.

"Stay there, I'll get help!" called Little Dragon. He soon came back with his friends, Prince Pip, Princess Pippa and Baron Boris. They were carrying a piece of rope to rescue the wagon.

Everybody helped, and they soon pulled the squeaky little wagon out of the bushes and back up onto the road.

"It's kind of old and smelly," said Pippa. "Let's give it a bath." So they pulled the wagon to his cave, and Little Dragon gave it a wash. Pip straightened the wheels.

Pippa painted it with
yellow dots. Then,
last of all, Boris
squirted some oil
onto its wheels.

"I wish I had a
wagon like yours,
Little Dragon!"said Pip.

"Oh, but it isn't mine," said Little
Dragon sadly, "I just found it. Now that it's fixed,
I'd better take it back again."

The mealtime trumpet sounded from the castle on the hill...
and Pip, Pippa and Boris had to hurry home for tea. Little
Dragon waved goodbye, then set off by himself to take the
wagon back down the hill. But the little wagon's wheels dug
into the ground and it squeaked even louder than before.

Little Dragon **pulled...** and **pulled...** but it was
hard work! So he sat down on the wagon for a rest. Suddenly
the wagon started to roll down the hill! Faster and faster it
went, steering around the curves as if by magic!

At last it stopped by the bush where Little Dragon found it.
Little Dragon waved goodbye and started to walk back up
the hill. He hadn't gone far when he heard a squeak. The
wagon was right behind him!

"Would you like to come home with me?" asked Little Dragon.

"Squeak!" went the wagon, which meant, "Yes, please!"

So the magic wagon gave him a ride all the way back home.

Follow the Trail

Once upon a time there was a pair of tiger cub twins called Tia and Timus. They lived on the edge of the jungle with their mother. One day, Tia asked their mother if they could go down to the waterhole on their own.

"Yes," agreed Mother Tiger. "But don't stray from the path."

So Tia and Timus headed straight for the waterhole and played happily in the shallows. As they were splashing around, they heard something hissing in the undergrowth.

"Hey, it's a snake," cried Timus. "Let's go snake hunting."

"Yes," cried Tia, leaping out of the water. And, forgetting all about their mother's warning, the two tiger cubs went charging deep into the jungle. They raced on and on until they were quite out of breath.

"I don't think we'll ever find that snake, do you?" laughed Tia.

"No," agreed Timus. "And now I'm hungry and tired. Let's go home."

But when the tiger cubs looked around they discovered that they were quite lost.

"Oh, no," wailed Tia. "We'll never find the path again."

"We should have remembered Mummy's warning," cried

Timus. The two cubs huddled together and trembled with fear.
They had heard all kinds of tales about the
dangers that lurked in the jungle.
Suddenly, Timus noticed
something on the ground.

"Look," he cried. "We've
left a trail of wet
footprints. All we need
to do is follow them and
we'll find our way back
to the waterhole."

"Then we'll be able to
find the path leading home,"
added Tia.

So the two tiger cubs very carefully
followed the footprint trail back to the waterhole. Then they
followed the path all the way home. They didn't even stop
when they heard something scratching around in a hollow
tree trunk.

They were so pleased when they saw their mother that they
bounced on her and gave her a big hug.

"Hey, what was that for?" asked Mother Tiger.

"Because we love you," said Tia.

"And you are so terribly wise," added Timus.

From then on, Tia and Timus always did exactly what their
mother told them.

Silent Snake

Silent snake coiled in the sun,
Can't hop, can't skip, can't jump, can't run.
She's got no legs, no feet nor hands,
But slides and slithers through the sands.

What Does the Donkey Say?

What does the donkey say?
Hee-haw, hee-haw.
What does the black bird say?
Caw-caw-caw.
What does the cat say?
Meow, meow, meow.
What does the dog say?
Bow-wow, bow-wow.

Prudence Stays Up

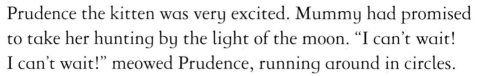

Prudence the kitten was very excited. Mummy had promised to take her hunting by the light of the moon. "I can't wait! I can't wait!" meowed Prudence, running around in circles.

"You can only go if you have a nap this afternoon," warned Mummy Cat. "Otherwise you'll be too tired."

But Prudence was much too excited to take a nap. As soon as her mother had gone she padded around the farm to tell all her friends.

"I'm a big girl now!" she boasted. "I'll be out until dawn."

By dusk everyone knew about the hunting trip, but Prudence was nowhere to be found. "Where can she be?" called Mummy Cat. Suddenly she heard a loud snoring sound coming from high up in a tree. She looked up, and there was Prudence, fast asleep. All the excitement had worn her out. There would be no night hunting for Prudence tonight.

"Never mind," smiled Mummy Cat. "There's always tomorrow!"

My Goat

My goat will eat most anything;
A pair of socks, some garden string,
A cardboard box, my favourite hat,
A bag of corn, the kitchen mat,
My brand new boots, a rubber ball,
He'll eat anything at all!
And if there's any room, at last...
He'll munch a bunch of fresh green grass.

Joey's Favourite Colour

One starry night Joey the polar bear cub and his friends were admiring the night sky. It was so colourful that even Joey and his friends were bathed in soft colours.

"Wow, it's beautiful!" gasped Joey.

"I've never seen such a purple sky," exclaimed Hare.

"Purple's my favourite colour," said Fox.

"And it's mine too," decided Hare. "What's your favourite colour, Joey?"

Joey scratched his head and frowned.

"I don't really know," he said finally. "I've never really thought about it before."

That night, while Joey was asleep, he had a wonderful dream

about a rainbow. The rainbow
was full of the brightest colours
you could imagine. They were
so lovely that Joey just couldn't
decide which one he liked best.

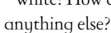

The next morning, Joey told his
mum about his dream.

"I just don't know which colour I like
best," he told his mum. "How can I decide?"

Mummy Polar Bear laughed. "You don't have to have a
favourite colour," she said kindly. "I like lots of colours because
they make me feel happy."

Joey looked around thoughtfully. He wondered what colours
made him feel happy. He loved all the bright colours of the
rainbow. But he couldn't decide which colour made him feel
the happiest.

That evening, as Joey snuggled up beside his mum he felt
happy and safe. And all of a sudden he
knew what his favourite colour was.
It was the colour of the snowy
world he lived in. It was the
colour of his two best friends.
And, best of all, it was the
colour of his lovely mum.
Joey's favourite colour was
white! How could it be
anything else?

A Tortoise

A tortoise is a funny thing,
And very lazy, too.
To eat and sleep the livelong day
Is all it cares to do.
And when I tried to make it race,
It wasn't any fun.
It tucked its head inside its shell
And simply wouldn't run.

Mr Mole

Oh, Mr Mole, come out of your hole,
And look at the sky so blue.
It must be dark deep under the ground,
And ever so lonely, too.
Oh, Mr Mole, come out of your hole,
Come out in the fresh clean air.
There's snails and bugs and bees that buzz...
and butterflies everywhere.
Oh, Mr Mole, come out of your hole,
And meet the world in the sun.
There's games to play and things to see.
Come out and have some fun!

Baby Bear

Brett was a baby bear cub who just couldn't wait to grow up into a big bear.

"I wish I was big and strong like Daddy," he told Mummy Bear one morning. "Then I could leave home and look after myself, just like a grown-up bear."

Mummy Bear smiled and ruffled Brett's furry little head.

"Don't be in such a hurry to grow up," she whispered. "You're my beautiful baby, and I love taking care of you."

"I'm not a baby," cried Brett. "I'm a big bear!"

And to show Mummy just how big he was, he leapt into the river and splashed around until, after a bit of a fight, he managed to catch a tiny, wriggling fish in his mouth.

"See," he cried triumphantly, proudly showing Mummy Bear what he had caught. "I can catch fish like a big grown-up bear."

"Well done," cried Mummy. Then she dipped a large paw into a pool and flipped out a huge fish.

"Oooh," gulped Little Bear. "I guess I've still got a bit to learn about fishing."

Mummy and Brett sat down beside the river and began to gnaw on their fish.

Suddenly, a large eagle began circling above them. He had a huge, curved beak, and razor-sharp claws.

Brett leapt to his feet and began waving his paws around wildly.

"Go away, you big brute!" he bellowed at the top of his voice. The eagle ignored him and prepared to dive.

Mummy Bear lifted up her head and gave a gentle growl. The eagle took one look at her sharp teeth and long claws and soared back up into the sky

"Oooh," gulped Little Bear. "I guess I've got a bit to learn about scaring eagles."

Mummy Bear smiled kindly. Then she picked up Brett and gave him a big, hairy hug.

"There's plenty of time to grow up. You should enjoy being my baby bear first."

"Yes," agreed Brett, snuggling up to his Mummy's warm, soft fur. "Being your baby is kind of nice, after all!"

Little Boy Blue

Little boy blue, come blow your horn,
The sheep's in the meadow, the cow's in the corn:
But where is the boy who looks after the sheep?
He's under the haystack fast asleep.
Will you wake him? No, not I,
For if I do, he's sure to cry.

Grig's Pig

Grandpa Grig
Had a pig,
In a field of clover;
Piggy died,
Grandpa cried,
And all the fun was over.

I Had a Little Hen

I had a little hen,
The prettiest ever seen.
She washed up all the dishes,
And kept the house so clean.
She went to the mill,
To fetch some flour.
And brought it home,
In less than an hour.

Hey Diddle Diddle

Hey diddle diddle,
The cat and the fiddle,
The cow jumped over the moon.
The little dog laughed to see such sport,
And the dish ran away with the spoon.

Over in the Meadow

Over in the meadow in the sand in the sun,
Lived an old mother toad and her little toadie one.
"Wink!" said the mother: "I wink!" said the one.
So they winked and they blinked in the sand in the sun.

Hickety Pickety

Hickety pickety, my black hen.
She lays eggs for gentlemen.
Sometimes nine and sometimes ten.
Hickety pickety, my black hen.

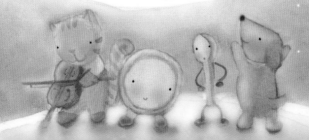

The Birds, the Beasts and the Bat

Once upon a time, the birds and the beasts had an argument and decided to fight one another. All the birds from miles around gathered together in the trees as they waited for the battle to begin.

"Whose side are you on?" the birds called to the bat, who was hanging by his feet from one of the branches.

"Yours, of course," replied the bat. "As you can see, I have wings, just like you."

Meanwhile, on the ground, the beasts were gathering. "Whose side are you on?" they shouted up to the bat.

"Yours, of course," the bat replied. "As you can see, I have fur and teeth, just like you."

The fierce battle began, and at first the birds were winning. Owls and eagles swooped down on mice and rabbits, and the bat was right behind them.

"I'm glad I am on your side," the bat told the birds.

Then the tables turned. Wolves, foxes and cats joined forces

to attack the birds, and as soon as he saw that the beasts were winning, the bat was right behind them.

"I'm glad I am on your side," the bat told the beasts.

Every time there was a break in the fighting, the bat flew back and forth between the birds and the beasts. One minute he was up in the trees, making up stories about what the beasts were planning, the next he was underground in the beasts' den, telling tales about the birds.

After some time, the birds and the beasts began to think that the battle might not be such a good idea after all.

A golden eagle made the first move. He flew down and spoke to a wolf, who was the leader of the beasts.

"The world is big enough for all of us," said the eagle. "There is no reason why we shouldn't all live happily, side by side."

"Let us live in peace," agreed the wolf.

The birds and the beasts were pleased that the fighting was over and began to celebrate. But as they talked about the battle, they realised that the bat had changed sides many times and had spread stories about everyone. Angrily, they turned on the bat, who quickly flew away. And ever since, the bat has hidden away in dark towers and deserted buildings during daylight, only daring to come out at night.

Aesop's moral: Someone who tries to trick others has no friends.

Muddypaws and the Birthday Party

Ben was just a smallish, normalish boy, but he was Muddypaws' best friend. They went out for the best splishy-splashy muddy walks together. They made new friends together of all sizes, colours and smells. They did everything together. But one sunny morning, Muddypaws woke up to find everything had changed in his house.

There were lots of new things! He sniffed about excitedly. What was happening? Where was Ben? He scampered off to find him.

"Woof!" barked Muddypaws, dropping his favourite ball at Ben's feet. "Let's play!"

But Ben was busy playing with a strange shiny thing. And the strange shiny thing was getting bigger... and bigger... and bigger...

Ben's new game looked like fun! Muddypaws pounced on the mountain of strange shiny things. BANG! Muddypaws jumped away as fast as he could. He didn't like that game!

But what was that delicious smell drifting over from
the kitchen...? His tail began to wag. It was hot dogs! Surely
no one would mind... if he just tried a little one? But someone
did mind!

"Bad dog!" scolded Ben's mum, and shooed him outside.

Muddypaws' tail stopped wagging at once. Why didn't Ben
want to play with him?
Why was everything
different today? Maybe
Honey the cat would
want to play.

"Woof!" barked
Muddypaws. "Let's go
and play!"

Honey turned up
her nose. She had better
things to do than play
with a puppy – like rolling on the grass in the sunshine!
Then the gate squeaked open... and the front garden was filled
with stamping feet, new smells and loud voices.

A crowd of children ran up the path into the house.
Something interesting was certainly going on and Muddypaws
was stuck in the garden with no one to play with. The flowers
were boring. The grass was boring. Even the smells were
boring. And Muddypaws was getting hungry.

He tried to find his bone... but it had disappeared.

What was happening inside the house? Maybe he would just look through the window to see.

Muddypaws pushed his nose up against the glass.

Ben and the other children were running around and laughing. They looked like they were having a great time! Muddypaws wanted to join in more than anything in the whole world. Then Ben's mum walked into the room carrying something that was twinkling brightly. It was the biggest, most delicious-looking cake Muddypaws had ever seen, and it was covered in little lights!

Muddypaws licked his lips and pressed his nose even harder against the window. Suddenly, the door opened. It was Ben.

"Mum says you can come in now!" cried Ben.

But all at once, Muddypaws didn't want to come inside.

He didn't like the big shiny things that went bang!

He didn't like it when Ben's mum shouted at him.

He wasn't sure about all the new children in his house. It was all so different from normal.

"I know what to do," Ben said.

Ben threw Muddypaws' ball high into the sky.

At once, Muddypaws forgot about the big shiny things...

He forgot about the new children...

He even forgot about Ben's mum shouting...

Ben wanted to play with him! Muddypaws jumped and barked for joy. He ran as fast as he could to fetch his ball, and brought it back to Ben.

Ben scooped Muddypaws into his arms and gave him a big hug.

"I'm so sorry, Muddypaws!" he whispered. "You didn't know it was my birthday. But you do know you're my best friend, don't you? And best friends do everything together, especially sharing birthday treats!"

"Woof!" barked Muddypaws happily, licking his lips. "Hot dogs!"

Little Dragon and the Birthday Surprise

Little Dragon was playing with Princess Pippa, Prince Pip and Baron Boris.

"It's great to have a real dragon for a friend!" said Pip.

"He's not a real dragon!" said Boris. "He can't breathe fire!"

"Yes, I can!" said Little Dragon angrily.

"Go on, Little Dragon, show him!" said Pippa.

Little Dragon tried… and tried… and tried! But nothing happened.

"Liar, liar, you can't breathe fire!" sang Boris. Little Dragon felt weary, teary and miserable.

"Never mind!" said Pippa. "I'm sure you'll be able to breathe fire when you're older."

"But when will I be older?" asked Little Dragon.

"On your birthday, of course!" said Pip.

"What's a birthday?" asked Little Dragon.

"You have them every year on the day that you were born," said Pip.

"But I wasn't born," sniffed Little Dragon. "I hatched!"

"When?" asked Pippa and Pip together.

"I don't know!" cried Little Dragon. "I was too little to tell the time!" He started to cry.

"Well," said Pippa, "if you haven't had a birthday yet, then it's about time you did! Tomorrow can be your birthday and we'll have a party with balloons, ice cream and games – and a big birthday cake with candles on the top!"

And that's exactly what they did. It was a wonderful party! There was music and dancing, funny games to play, lots of yummy things to eat, and a pile of presents for Little Dragon! Then the magic wagon brought in the birthday cake and everyone sang, "Happy birthday to you!"

"Oh, no!" cried Princess Pippa. "Who will light the candles! How can Little Dragon blow them out and make a wish?"

"Don't worry," said Little Dragon. "I'll blow on them anyway, just for luck!"

He took a big breath, then… Little Dragon's birthday wish came true! His fiery breath lit all the candles in one go!

Baron Boris was a bit scared, but everybody else cheered.

"Yippee!" shouted Little Dragon. **"I do like birthdays!"**

Apple Picking

One day, Gloria the pig was feeling hungry. She gazed at the juicy red apples on the tree on the other side of the wall. They looked delicious! The problem was, Gloria was just too small to reach them.

"Maybe I could grab one from up on the wall," she thought, scrambling up. CRASH! Gloria fell to the ground.

"Maybe I can knock one down with this stick," she oinked, waving it in the air. But she just ended up covered in leaves.

"Maybe you can peck one down, Magpie," suggested Gloria. Magpie tried his best, but that didn't work either. The apples kept falling on the wrong side of the wall.

"I give up," sighed Gloria. Just then, Farmer Sam arrived.

"You look fed up, Gloria," he said. "What can I do to cheer you up?"

Farmer Sam looked around and then had a brilliant idea. He went into the orchard, picked a bucketful of juicy red apples, and poured them into Gloria's trough.

Gloria squealed with delight. She was as happy as a pig in an orchard!

The Thrush

It was winter, and Tufty the thrush's garden home
was full of joy. There were juicy worms to eat and
five lively children to watch as they played in
the snow. She even enjoyed the games
of chase she played with the
cat next door.

But when spring arrived,
Tufty realised that she needed
somewhere quiet to build her
nest – somewhere peaceful and
safe, away from the playful cat.
Tufty searched until she found
the perfect place in an old teapot on a shelf in the shed.

One day, the children banged into the shed in search
of a ball. The tallest boy saw the nest right away.

"Ooooh! Our thrush has made a nest," he said. "Let's leave
her alone and close the door so that Kitty can't get in."

A few days later the eggs hatched, and Tufty had five
perfect babies of her own. It wasn't long before they were ready
to make their first trip into the garden.

One by one, Tufty led her brood outside to munch on juicy
worms and watch the children play.

"Look at our thrush's new family!" cried the
children. "Aren't they the prettiest chicks you have ever seen!"

Tufty was so proud, she sang her heart out!

How the Bear Lost His Tail

Once upon a time, the bear had a long, black, glossy tail, and the fox was very jealous of it.

"What makes Bear think his tail is so wonderful?" growled the fox to himself. "My tail is much finer than his. I'm going to teach him a lesson."

It was winter, and all the lakes were covered with thick ice. The fox made a hole in the ice and surrounded it with fat, tasty-looking fish. That evening, when the bear passed by, the fox dangled his tail through the hole into the water.

"What are you doing?" the bear asked.

"I am fishing," the fox replied. "Would you like to try?"

The bear loved to eat fish, so he was very eager to try.

"As you can see, I have caught all the fish in this spot," the fox told him. "Let's go over there and make a new hole."

They walked over to a shallow part of the lake, and the fox

cut a hole in the ice.

"This is what you must do," the fox explained. "Turn your back to the hole and don't think about fish at all – otherwise they will sense that you are trying to catch them and they won't come near. Soon a fish will grab your tail, then you can pull it out. In the meantime you must be very patient and stay perfectly still."

The bear put his long tail through the hole in the ice and did exactly as the fox had told him.

The next morning, the fox went back to the lake and saw that the bear was still sitting on the ice. He was fast asleep and covered in snow. The hole had frozen over during the night and now the bear's tail was trapped in the ice.

"You've caught a fish! Pull out your tail!" cried the fox.

The bear woke up with a start and tugged his tail as hard as he could. All of a sudden, there was a loud CRACK! as the bear's frozen tail snapped off.

And that explains why bears have very short tails and why they are definitely not friends with foxes.

A Long-Tail'd Pig

A long-tail'd pig,
Or a short-tail'd pig,
Or a pig without a tail?
A sow-pig, or a boar-pig,
Or a pig with a curly tail?

If Wishes Were Horses

If wishes were horses,
Beggars would ride.
If turnips were watches,
I would wear one by my side.

Fuzzy Wuzzy

Fuzzy Wuzzy was a bear,
Fuzzy Wuzzy had no hair,
Fuzzy Wuzzy wasn't
Really fuzzy, wuzzy?

Mousie

Mousie comes a-creeping, creeping.
Mousie comes a-peeping, peeping.
Mousie says, "I'd like to stay,
But I haven't time today."
Mousie pops into his hole,
And says, "Achoo! I've caught a cold!"

In April

In April's sweet month,
When leaves start to spring,
Lambs skip like fairies,
And birds build and sing.

Horsey, Horsey

Horsey, horsey, don't you stop,
Just let your feet go clippety clop,
The tail goes swish and the wheels go round,
Giddy up, we're homeward bound!

Ebony

Once upon a time there was a beautiful young horse called Ebony. He was as black as midnight, with a white star in the middle of his forehead. Ebony was the only black horse in his herd and was very proud of his good looks.

Ebony lived on a wild moor with the rest of the herd. They had a wonderful life roaming free. They would gallop through the bogs, munch on gorse and do exactly as they pleased. Ebony should have been very happy but he was always dreaming of a better life.

"I'm so handsome," he would boast. "I feel sure that I am destined for better things."

One day, Ebony saw a grand coach passing by. It was pulled by four black horses – but not one of them was as handsome as Ebony.

"What a fine thing it would be to pull a coach like that," sighed Ebony, as he watched the coach pass by.

Suddenly, Ebony had an idea. He would follow the coach and see if he could make friends with the four black horses that pulled it. Maybe they could tell him how to become a fine horse like them.

So, with a brief neigh, Ebony wished farewell to the rest of the herd and trotted off down the road.

Ebony followed the coach and horses until they reached a small village, where he was soon spotted by a country farmer who was passing by.

"What a beautiful creature," exclaimed the farmer, who was called Farmer Jones. And he quickly caught the wild horse and took him home.

Ebony was turned out into a small paddock with an old carthorse called Fred, and his new life – and his training – began. Before long he was pulling his new master and his family in a small trap.

Of course, it wasn't the fine coach Ebony had dreamt of, and Ebony was still sure he was destined for better things, but he enjoyed pulling the trap and sharing the paddock with Fred – even if the old carthorse was a little on the rough side.

After Ebony had been pulling the trap for some months, a saddle was put on his back for the first time, and he was broken to ride. After that, he regularly took Farmer Jones into market. But the thing Ebony loved best was taking Farmer Jones hunting, and he soon became one of the finest horses in the county. He could gallop faster than any other, and jump higher than most. He was so handsome and powerful that he was admired by everyone.

One day, a fine coach pulled up outside the farm and a well-dressed gentleman and noisy girl jumped out. They had heard about Ebony, and had come to buy him for a large bag of gold. Ebony was thrilled. Now at last he would live the life he deserved!

Ebony was taken to a grand house. At first he was excited, but when he saw his new home he was shocked. It was a dark and dirty stable. His stablemates, who pulled the fine coach, were so grumpy that really he only had the rats for company.

Every day, Ebony was taken out of the stable and a hard saddle was thumped on his back. Then the noisy girl would leap onto his back. She would yank him in the mouth and thump him in the sides with her sharp heels. Then she would gallop him without mercy and jump him over everything from rusty barbed wire fences to long forgotten ploughs.

The years passed and Ebony changed. He grew skinny and his fine black coat lost its shine. He could no longer gallop and jump as he had before. One day, the noisy young girl decided she didn't like him any more.

"I **want** a new horse," she told her father.

So Ebony was sent to market, where no one gave him a second glance.

Luckily for Ebony, a familiar figure appeared before the end of the day and rubbed him on the head. It was Farmer Jones. The kind farmer bought Ebony for just a few silver coins and led him away. But he didn't take him back to the farm. Instead, he led Ebony up to a wild place and let him go.

At first Ebony was scared, but then he saw a familiar rock. He sniffed the air and looked around him. In the distance he could see a herd of horses. He neighed and one of the horses neighed back. Ebony kicked up his heels and galloped away from Farmer Jones. He was home at last. And after all his adventures, he finally knew that the wild moors were the best place in the world.

The Old Woman and the Fat Hen

An old woman kept a hen that laid one egg every morning without fail. The eggs were large and delicious, and the old woman was able to sell them for a very good price at market.

"If my hen would lay two eggs every day," she said to herself, "I would be able to earn twice as much money!"

The old woman decided that the best way to make the hen lay an extra egg each day was to feed her twice as much. So besides giving the hen a bowl of corn in the morning, the woman gave her one every evening, too.

The hen was very happy and gobbled up all the extra corn.

Each day the old woman went to the henhouse expecting to find two eggs, but there was still only one – even though the hen was getting fatter and fatter. One morning, the woman looked in the nest box and there were no eggs at all. There were none the next day either, nor any day after that. All the extra food had made the hen so fat and contented that she had become lazy and had given up laying eggs altogether!

Aesop's moral: Things don't always work out as planned.

The Mice in Council

Once there was a family of mice. They would have been very happy, if it weren't for the cat who also lived in their house. Every time they crept into the kitchen to pick up a few crumbs, the cat would pounce, and chase them under the floorboards.

"If we don't do something soon, we'll starve," said the oldest mouse. "We must hold a council to decide on a plan."

All the mice got together, but none of them could come up with an idea that they all agreed on. Finally, the youngest mouse had a brainwave. "We can put a bell on the cat's collar, so we can hear him coming," he said.

The mice agreed that it was an excellent plan, and the young mouse felt very **proud** of himself. Then the grandfather mouse stood up. "You are a very smart young fellow to come up with such an idea," he said, "but, tell me this – who is going to be brave enough to put the bell on the cat's collar?"

Aesop's moral: It is sometimes easy to think of a clever plan, but it can be much more difficult to carry it out.

Bow Wow

Bow wow, says the dog,
Mew, mew, says the cat,
Grunt, grunt, goes the hog,
And squeak goes the rat.
Chirp, chirp, says the sparrow,
Caw, caw, says the crow,
Quack, quack, says the duck,
What cuckoos say you know.

So, with sparrows and cuckoos,
With rats and with dogs,
With ducks and with crows,
With cats and with hogs,

A fine song I have made
To please you my dear,
And if it's well sung
'Twill be charming to hear.

Six Little Mice

Six little mice sat down to spin,
Kitty passed by and she peeped in.
"What are you doing, my little men?"
"Making coats for gentlemen."
"Shall I come in and cut off your threads?"
"No, no, Mistress Kitty, you'd bite off our heads."
"Oh, no, I'll not; I'll help you to spin."
"That may be so, but you can't come in."
Says Kitty: "You look so wondrous wise,
I like your whiskers and bright black eyes;
Your house is the nicest house I see,
I think there is room for you and for me."
The mice were so pleased that they opened the door,
And Kitty soon had them all caught on the floor.

The Three Little Pigs

Once upon a time, there were three little pigs. One day, it was time for them to leave home and build houses of their own.

"Watch out for the big bad wolf," warned their mother, as she watched them trot off down the road.

After a while, the three little pigs met a man carrying bundles of straw. So the first little pig bought some and used them to build his very own straw house.

Meanwhile, the second little pig bought a stack of sticks from a woodcutter and began to build a stick house.

The third little pig, who was the smartest of the bunch, bought a load of bricks from a builder and set to work building a fine strong house of bricks.

The next morning, the first little pig was sitting in his straw house when the big bad wolf came along.

"Little pig, let me in!" growled the wolf, peering in.

"Not by the hairs on my chinny chin chin!" replied the piggy.

"Then I'll huff and I'll puff and I'll blow your house down!" growled the wolf. And that's just what he did.

"Help!" squealed the first little pig, running down the road.
Next, the wolf visited the stick house.

"Little pig, let me in!" he called.

"Not by the hairs on my chinny chin chin!" cried the piggy.

"Then I'll huff and I'll puff and I'll blow your house down!"
growled the wolf, and that's exactly what he did.

"Oh, my!" cried the second little pig, running down the road.

When the third little pig saw his brother and sister being
chased by the wolf, he quickly let them in and shut the door.

"Little pigs, let me in!" roared the angry wolf.

"Not by the hairs on our chinny chin chins!" cried the pigs.

"Then I'll huff and I'll puff and I'll blow your house down!"
cried the wolf. So he huffed and he puffed... but the fine
strong house of bricks did not fall down. "I'm coming down
the chimney to gobble you up!"
shouted the furious wolf.

As the wolf climbed onto the roof,
the three little pigs heaved a big
pot of water onto the fire. Then
they waited.

WHOOSH! The wolf slid
down the chimney and landed
with a splash in the boiling water.

"YOUCH!" he howled.
And he raced out of the kitchen
as fast as his paws would carry
him – never to be seen again!

Jungle Hide-and-Seek

One day Little Elephant was walking through the jungle.
He hadn't gone far when he bumped into Giraffe.

"Hello," called Little Elephant. "Do you want to play?"

Giraffe peered down at Little Elephant and smiled.

"Okay," he said. "You can play hide-and-seek with me, Zebra
and Crocodile. Close your eyes and count to one hundred, then
come and find us."

So Little Elephant closed his eyes and counted to one hundred,
which took a very long time because he was only a very little
elephant. Finally, he opened his eyes and began to search the
jungle for his friends.

He searched through the long grass but he didn't see Zebra
hiding among the tall blades. He searched among the acacia
trees but he didn't see Giraffe hiding between the tree trunks.

He searched the watering
hole but he didn't see
Crocodile hiding in the
shallows. He searched and
searched but he couldn't
find any of his friends.
By midday, Elephant
was feeling so sad that he
decided to call it a day.

"I give up," he shouted.
"You are all too good at

hiding for me."

Then he lay down among some rocks to rest.

One by one, Giraffe, Zebra and Crocodile crept out of their hiding places and went in search of Little Elephant. But they couldn't find him anywhere.

They made so much noise stomping around that Little Elephant woke up and groaned.

"Hey, that rock just groaned," gasped Giraffe.

"I'm not a rock," said Little Elephant. "It's me, Little Elephant."

"So it is!" cried Zebra.

"That's amazing," smiled Crocodile. "Your grey skin makes it hard to see you when you are hiding among the rocks. Just like my green skin helps me to hide in the watering hole."

"And my stripes help me hide in the long grass," said Zebra.

"And my patches help me hide among the tall trees," said Giraffe.

"Hooray," cried Little Elephant happily. "I'm good at hiding – just like you!"

The Wolf and the Crane

Once upon a time a greedy wolf was gobbling up an enormous meal when he got a bone caught in his throat. The wolf tried coughing… then he tried swallowing… then he tried drinking, but the bone would not move up or down. It was well and truly stuck, and he couldn't eat a thing. As the days passed, the wolf got thinner and thinner.

One morning, the wolf noticed a crane flying overhead and he had an idea.

"You have such a wonderful long bill," he said to her, when she had landed. "You could do me **a great service** and save my life. I have a bone caught in my throat, so I cannot eat, and I am starving. With your long beak, you could reach down into my throat and pull the bone out for me."

The crane felt very nervous about putting her head into a hungry wolf's mouth After all, he could be planning to eat her.

"I'd like to help," the crane replied, "but I'm afraid that you might bite my head off."

"Why would I do that?" the wolf replied innocently. "In fact, I'd be so grateful to you that I would give you a reward."

The crane was tempted by the thought of a reward, so she agreed to do as the wolf asked.

The wolf opened his mouth, and the crane reached down into his throat with her long bill. She was relieved to find that the wolf was telling the truth and that he really did have a bone stuck there. So she grabbed it with her beak and pulled it out.

As soon as the crane had pulled out the bone, the wolf turned around and began to walk away.

"Just a minute! What about my reward?" called the crane.

"I've given you your reward already," the wolf replied. "I let you take your head out of my mouth without biting it off, even though I am starving. You should be very grateful for that!"

Aesop's moral: Never expect a reward for helping the wicked.

The Mice and the Douglas Fir Cones

Long ago, a family of mice lived in a forest. It was a wonderful place to live, with plenty of nuts and berries to eat, but there was one problem. A fox also lived in the forest, and he was always trying to catch them for his supper.

Finally the mice came up with a plan. One of them would keep watch, while the other mice gathered food. That way, if the fox came along, the mouse on guard would give a squeak of alarm and the family could race back to their home beneath the Douglas fir tree.

The plan worked well, until one day the youngest mouse took his turn as lookout. He soon got bored keeping watch for the fox, and after a while he began chatting to a frog who was hopping around under the tree.

Soon the conversation turned to the forest and the animals that lived there, until at last the fox's name was mentioned.

"I am very pleased that you and your family live here now," croaked the frog.

"I used to have a lot of trouble with that sly old fox – but he much prefers eating mice to frogs, so he doesn't bother me any more."

Suddenly the little mouse remembered that he was supposed to be watching out for the fox. He took a quick look around and, to his horror, he spotted the sly creature hiding beneath the branches of the Douglas fir tree. Worse still, the fox had his beady eye on the mouse's unsuspecting family, who were busy gathering food. He was ready to pounce!

"Run! It's the fox!" squeaked the little mouse at the top of his voice – but it was too late. The mice scampered around frantically, searching for somewhere to hide.

All at once, the father mouse saw that the ground around the tree was covered with Douglas fir cones. "Hide in the cones!" he squeaked, squeezing in between the fir cones' scales as far as he could.

The fox was very confused. One moment the ground was covered with fleeing mice – the next moment they had all disappeared! He didn't think of looking at the fir cones scattered around. But we know what happened, don't we? And to this very day, if you look at a Douglas fir cone you can still see the hind legs and the tails of the mice sticking out.

Yankee Doodle

Yankee Doodle went to town,
Riding on a pony;
He stuck a feather in his cap
And called it macaroni.

Yankee Doodle keep it up,
Yankee Doodle dandy,
Mind the music and the step,
And with the girls be handy.

Snorri Pig

Snorri pig had a curly tail.
A curly tail, a curly tail,
His head was round as the top of a pail,
Hey up for Snorri pig!

Snorri pig had big brown eyes,
Big brown eyes, big brown eyes,
And he was lord of all the sties,
Hey up for Snorri pig!

When Snorri pig met a lady sow,
A lady sow, a lady sow,
He'd smile and bend his knees full low,
Hey up for Snorri pig!
But when he met another boar,
Another boar, another boar,
He'd tread him into the farmyard floor,
Hey up for Snorri pig!

Squirrel's Nut Pile

One morning, Squirrel scurried around the forest floor. He scampered up trees and then down again. His bushy tail swayed from side to side as he went. He was busy gathering nuts for the winter. When he had collected a big pile, he stopped and scratched his furry ears.

"Now I just need to find somewhere safe to store them," he muttered, looking around. "Somewhere warm and dry and not too far away. And somewhere where the pesky weasels won't find them."

As he peered around hopefully, Rabbit popped up from a hole in the ground. She twitched her nose and smiled at Squirrel.

"Aha," thought Squirrel. "That looks like the perfect place."

"Hello, Rabbit," he called. "Can I store my nuts in your burrow?"

Rabbit shook her head sadly. "Sorry," she replied. "But there won't be enough room for all my babies and all your nuts.

I've just moved out of my old burrow in the beech tree because it was too small for us all."

Squirrel sighed and looked very disappointed. Rabbit felt so sorry for him that she wondered what she could do to help. There must be somewhere Squirrel could keep his nuts. She thought and thought until she had a brilliant idea.

"I know," she cried, thumping her foot with excitement. "Why don't you use my old burrow in the beech tree. It's warm, dry and surely big enough for all your nuts."

"Oh, thank you," cried Squirrel. "That will be perfect. The weasels will never think of looking there, and it's only a hop and skip from my nest,"

After kissing Rabbit on her fluffy cheek, Squirrel scampered away and began storing his nuts in their new hide-away. But he didn't hide every single one of them. He made sure there was a nice big pile for kind Rabbit and her family. After all, **one good turn deserves another.**

As I Was Going to St Ives

As I was going to St Ives,
I met a man with seven wives,
Each wife had seven sacks,
Each sack had seven cats,
Each cat had seven kits;
Kits, cats, sacks and wives,
How many were going to St Ives?

Tom, Tom, the Piper's Son

Tom, Tom, the piper's son,
Stole a pig and away he ran.
The pig was eat and Tom was beat,
And Tom went roaring down the street.

Two Little Dicky Birds

Two little dicky birds sitting on a wall,
One named Peter, one named Paul.
Fly away, Peter! Fly away, Paul!
Come back, Peter! Come back, Paul!

Hurt No Living Thing

Hurt no living thing:
Ladybird, nor butterfly,
Nor moth with dusty wing,
Nor cricket chirping cheerily,
Nor grasshopper so light of leap,
Nor dancing gnat, nor beetle fat,
Nor harmless worms that creep.

Two Little Dogs

Two little dogs
Sat by the fire,
Over a fender of coal dust;
Said one little dog
To the other little dog,
"If you don't talk,
Why, I must."

The Horse and Rider

The prairie blows the grasses
And whips the horse's mane.
They travel, horse and rider,
Through the sea of amber grain.

The Open Road

"Ratty," said Mole, one bright summer morning, "I want to ask you a favour."

"Why, certainly," said Ratty, who was sitting by the river.

"Well, what I wanted to ask you is, can we call on Mr Toad? I've heard so much about him."

"Get the boat out and we'll paddle up there at once. Toad is always in and will be delighted to meet you."

Rat and Mole rounded a bend in the river and came in sight of a handsome old stone house.

"There's Toad Hall," said Ratty. "It is the biggest house in these parts."

They moored the boat on the bank and started to walk towards Toad Hall.

"Hooray!" cried Toad as the three animals shook paws.

"The very fellows I wanted to see! You've got to help me sort out something really important!"

"It's about boating, I suppose?" asked the Rat.

"Forget about that!" cried the Toad. "I gave that up ages ago.

Now I've discovered the **real** thing. Come with me!"

He led the way to the stable yard, where, in the open, was a shiny new gypsy caravan with red wheels.

"There!" cried Toad. "There's the **real** life. A home away from home, travelling the road without a care in the world."

Mole followed Toad up the steps and inside. Ratty remained where he was, hands thrust deep in his pockets.

"I've thought of everything," cried Toad. He pulled open a cupboard. "Here's everything we could possibly want to eat."

He threw open another cupboard. "Here's all the clothes we need! We must start at once."

"I beg your pardon," said Rat, "but did I hear you say *we?*"

"Now, dear Ratty," said Toad calmly, "don't get on your high horse. You've got to come."

"I'm not coming, and that is that," said the Rat.

"Me neither," said Mole, siding loyally with Ratty.

"All the same…" he added, "it does sound like fun."

"I'll say it would be fun," said Toad, and he began to paint the joys of caravanning. In no time at all, even Rat was interested.

And so it was that all three friends set off that afternoon to discover the joys of caravanning on the open road.

"This is the life, eh!" said a sleepy Toad that evening, when they stopped for supper. "Better than talking about your river, eh, Ratty?"

"I don't talk about my river, Toad," replied Rat. "You know I don't. But I think about it," he added quietly, "all the time."

Mole reached out and squeezed Ratty's paw. "Dear Ratty," he whispered. "Should we run away tomorrow and go back to our dear old hole on the river?"

"No, we'll see it out," whispered the Rat. "We must stick by Toad until he's over this craze. It won't take long."

The end was nearer than even Rat suspected. Next morning, Mole turned the horse's head onto their first really wide main road. In the distance they heard a faint warning hum, like the buzz of a bee. An instant later, with a loud BEEP!, a whirl of wind, and a blast of sound, a motor car tore past.

The old horse who was pulling the caravan let out a whinny of fear, reared, then plunged and bucked, driving the caravan into a ditch, where it landed with a huge crash.

Ratty danced with rage. "You villains!" he shouted, shaking both fists. "You scoundrels, you… you… road hogs!"

Mole looked down at the caravan. Panels and windows were smashed, the axles hopelessly bent, and cans of food were scattered about. And Toad? Toad sat in the middle of the road staring in the direction of the now disappeared car.

Rat shook him by the shoulder. "Come on, Toad, do get up!"

But Toad wouldn't move. "Glorious!" he murmured. "That's the way to travel. Oh, bliss! Oh, beep beep!"

"Oh, drat Toad!" said Ratty crossly. "I'm done with him! I've seen it all before. He's off onto a new craze. He'll be in a dream for days. We'll just have to get him to his feet, then make our way to the nearest town and catch a train home."

"Now, look here, Toad!" said Ratty. "You'll have to make a complaint against that scoundrel and his car."

"Me? Complain?" murmured Toad. "I wouldn't dream of it. I'm going to order one right away!"

Ratty sighed. Some things would never change.

High Diddle Doubt

High diddle doubt, my candle's out,
And my little dame's not at home:
So saddle my hog, and bridle my dog,
And fetch my little dame home.

My Kitten

Hey, my kitten, my kitten,
And hey, my kitten, my deary,
Such a sweet little pet as this
I love to have so near me.

On the Grassy Banks

On the grassy banks,
Lambkins at their pranks;
Woolly sisters, woolly brothers,
Jumping off their feet,
While their woolly mothers
Watch over them and bleat.

The Little Bird

This little bird flaps its wings,
Flaps its wings, flaps its wings,
This little bird flaps its wings,
And flies away in the morning!

Purple Cow

I never saw a purple cow.
I never hope to see one.
But I can tell you, anyhow,
I'd rather see than be one!

Pretty Little Goldfish

Pretty little goldfish
Never can talk.
All it does is wiggle
When it tries to walk.

How the Cardinal Bird Got His Colour

Once upon a time, there was a raccoon who loved to tease his neighbour, the wolf. The raccoon would pull the wolf's tail, then run away, hide up a tree, and drop pine cones on the wolf's head. And when the wolf was asleep he would tickle his nose with a feather until he sneezed.

One day the wolf got so angry with the raccoon that he chased him through the forest. When the raccoon reached the river, he climbed up into the branches of a tall tree and waited to see what the wolf would do.

The wolf saw the raccoon's reflection in the water, so he jumped into the river to catch him. But the raccoon had disappeared!

"He must be under the water," thought the wolf, diving down to search the riverbed.

Finally, exhausted from his efforts, the wolf climbed onto the bank and fell into a deep sleep.

As soon as the wolf was snoring, the raccoon came down from the tree to play yet another trick on the poor wolf. He got some mud from the river and stuck it all over the wolf's eyes. When the wolf woke up, he couldn't open his eyes.

"Help!" he cried. "I can't see! I've gone blind!"

A brown bird, who was perched in the branches of the tree, took pity on the wolf.

"I am just a little brown bird," he said. "Everyone says that I am very dull and boring, but I will help you if I can."

The bird flew down and carefully picked the dried mud from the wolf's eyes until he could open them.

"Thank you," said the wolf. "Now I would like to do something for you in return. Please follow me."

The wolf led the bird to a rock that oozed red dye. He took a twig and chewed it until the end was like a paintbrush, then he dipped it into the red dye and painted the brown bird's feathers a glorious red colour.

"From now on you will be known as the cardinal bird in honour of your beautiful red plumage," the wolf told him.

The bird was very proud of his colourful feathers – no one would ever call him dull and boring again.

And that is how the beautiful cardinal bird got his colour.

Bees Sneeze

The bees
Sneeze and wheeze,
Scraping pollen and honey
From the lime trees.

The ant
Hurries and pants,
Storing up everything
it wants.

But I lie and sigh,
Watching all
The bugs go by!

The Derby Ram

As I was going to Derby all on a market day,
I met the finest ram, sir, that ever was fed upon hay;
Upon hay, upon hay, upon hay;
I met the finest ram, sir, that ever was fed upon hay.

This ram was fat behind, sir; this ram was fat before;
This ram was ten yards round, sir; indeed, he was no more;
No more, no more, no more;
This ram was ten yards round, sir; indeed, he was no more.

The horns that grew on his head, they were so wondrous high,
As I've been plainly told, sir; they reached up to the sky.
The sky, the sky, the sky;
As I've been plainly told, sir, they reached up to the sky.

The tail that grew from his back, sir, was six yards and an ell;
And it was sent to Derby to toll the market bell;
The bell, the bell, the bell;
And it was sent to Derby to toll the market bell.

Little Dragon Goes to School

Little Dragon bounced out of bed. Today was his very first day of school! He was a little bit excited. First, he had a big bowl of breakfast, then he washed, sploshed and brushed his teeth.

School was big, and Little Dragon felt very little. Then he saw his best friends, Prince Pip and Princess Pippa.

"Hello, it's me!" said Little Dragon.

"Get to the back of the line!" said Little Baron Boris.

When the bell rang, they all went inside. There was a row of coat pegs with little pictures over them. Little Dragon liked the piggy peg.

"That's my peg!" said Little Baron Boris. "Get your own!"

So Little Dragon hung his bag on the spider peg instead. They all sat in a circle and the nice teacher, Miss Plum, called out their names.

"Little Dragon?" she said.

"Hello, it's me!" said Little Dragon. Everyone giggled. Miss Plum showed them how to write their names.

Little Dragon **tried...** and **tried**... but ... it was tricky!

Soon it was time for lunch.

"I've forgotten my lunch!" said Little Dragon.

"You can share our sandwiches – we've got lots!" said Pip and Pippa.

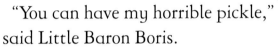

"You can have my horrible pickle," said Little Baron Boris.

After lunch they did painting. Prince Pip painted a tiger. Princess Pippa painted a flower. Little Dragon painted Boris's bottom and a pink pig!

When everybody was clean again they all sat down. Then Miss Plum read them a funny story about a big bad troll and a clever little goat. Little Dragon felt happy and sleepy.

Soon it was time to go home. Little Dragon found his spider peg and got his bag. He said goodbye to Miss Plum and went outside.

Little Dragon started to cry.

"I wish I could come to school again tomorrow," he sniffled.

"You can!" said Pippa, "Every day except for holidays!"

"Yippee!" shouted Little Dragon. "I like school!"

The Swallow and the Crow

One day, a young swallow landed on a branch next to a wise old crow. The swallow looked down his nose at the crow and said, "I don't think much of your feathers. You should take more **pride** in your appearance."

The old crow was very angry at being criticised by this **rude** young bird and was about to fly away in disgust, when the swallow continued, "Look at me with my bright, soft, downy feathers. These are the sort of feathers a **well-dressed** bird needs. Those stiff, black quills of yours are not worth having."

"Those soft feathers of yours might be all right in the spring and summer," the crow replied. "But I don't remember seeing you around here in the winter, when the trees are full of ripe berries. Winter is my favourite time of year, and I am very grateful for my stiff, black feathers then, because they keep me warm and dry. What use are your fancy feathers then?"

Aesop's moral: Fine weather friends are not worth much.

The Ant and the Dove

One morning, a thirsty ant crawled down to the edge of a river to take a drink. As he was quenching his thirst, a boat passed by, making waves. SWOOSH! The waves swept the poor ant into the water and carried him downstream.

Luckily, a kind dove sitting in a tree on the riverbank saw what was happening. Quick as a flash, she dropped a leaf into the water near the ant, who was able to climb on to it and float back to the shore.

A little later, the ant was drying off in the sun when he saw a bird-catcher heading for the river with his net. Very slowly, the man crept up to the tree where the dove was sitting and quietly laid out his net to trap her. The ant was determined to help the kind creature who had saved his life, so he opened his jaws and bit the bird-catcher on the foot.

"Ouch!" yelled the man loudly. Startled by the loud noise, the dove flew away, and was saved from the bird-catcher's net!

Aesop's moral:
One good turn
deserves another.

The Bottom of the Sea

See, see, what can you see?
What can you see
At the bottom of the sea?
Shoals of fish that shimmer and shine,
Twisting, turning, all in time,
Yellow, red and stripy, too.
Fish of every shape and hue.
See, see, that's what you see.
That's what you see
At the bottom of the sea.

See, see, what can you see?
What can you see
At the bottom of the sea?
A coral reef far below,
Where pink anemones bloom and grow.
Crabs and starfish call it home,
And curious seahorses love to roam.
See, see, that's what you see.
That's what you see
At the bottom of the sea.

The Hungry Toad

"Croak!" said the toad, "I'm hungry, I think,
Today I've had nothing to eat or to drink.
I'll crawl to a garden and jump through the pails,
And there I'll dine nicely on slugs and on snails."

At the Zoo

At the zoo we saw a bear.
He had long, dark, fuzzy hair
We saw a lion in a cage.
He was in an awful rage!
We saw the big, long-necked giraffe,
And the silly monkeys made us laugh.
But my favourite animal at the zoo
Is the elephant – how about you?

Billy Pringle's Pig

Billy Pringle had a little pig,
When it was young...
It was not very big,
When it was old...
It lived in clover,
Now it's gone
And that's all over.

Butterfly, Butterfly

"Butterfly, butterfly,
Where do you go?"
"Where the sun shines,
And where the buds grow."

Bossy Cow

"Bossy cow, bossy cow, where do you lie?"
"In the green meadow, under the sky."
"Billy-horse, billy-horse, where do you lie?"
"Out in the stable with nobody nigh."
"Birdies bright, birdies sweet, where do you lie?"
"Up in the treetops, oh, ever so high!"
"Baby dear, baby love, where do you lie?"
"In my warm crib, with Mamma close by."

The Sparrow

A little cock-sparrow sat on a green tree,
And he chirruped, he chirruped, so merry was he;
A naughty boy came with his wee bow and arrow,
Determined to shoot this little cock-sparrow.
"This little cock-sparrow shall make me a stew,
And I shall make me a little pie, too."
"Oh, no," says the sparrow, "I won't make a stew."
So he flapped his wings and away he flew.

That's Not My Dad!

Patty and Dad were on top of a hill,
when Patty said, "Dad! Let's
slide down for a thrill!"
"OK!" hollered Dad,
and with great
whoops of delight...
he whizzed round the
corner, right out of sight.
"Where's my
dad?" cried Patty.
"Lost your dad?"
asked Puffin. "Don't
fret, little bear.
He slid right behind
that enormous rock
over there."

All alone, looking nervously over her shoulder,
Patty crept up to the ice-covered boulder.
"There he is!" Patty cried, spying whiskers and snout.
"That's definitely Dad – there's his nose sticking out!"
But it was Walrus. "That's not my dad!" she cried.
"Lost your dad?" wobbled Walrus. "Why, isn't that him?
I know how you polar bears all love to swim."
Patty skipped off to the steep, icy ledge,
and carefully poked her nose over the edge.

"There he is!" exclaimed Patty. "That walrus was right!"
And up bobbed a shape that was furry and white.
 But it was Seal. **"That's not my dad!"** cried Patty.
 "Lost your dad?" asked Seal. "He's not far," said her daughter.
"We just heard him singing down there in the water."
 Patty dived into the sea and thought, "Brrr!
The water is freezing! I'm glad I've got fur!"

"There he is!" Patty bubbled. "That's him swimming along.
It sounds like his big, deep voice humming a song!"
 But it was Whale! **"That's not my dad!"** cried Patty.
 "Lost your dad?" wondered Whale. "If you want my advice,
you'll look over there by that hole in the ice."
 Under the ice the cold ocean seemed vast...
and all Patty's paws were soon paddling fast.
 Then through the round hole she glimpsed eyes and a nose.
 "There he is!" she thought. "Looking for me, I suppose!"
But it was Fox. **"That's not my dad!"** cried Patty.
 "Lost your dad?" asked Fox. "I know where to go.

He's up on that bank, digging holes in the snow."
   The snowflakes were falling, but Patty was swift...
as she climbed to the top of the deep snowy drift.
   She heard something scrabbling, then up popped an ear.
   "There he is!" Patty cried. "Fox was right, Dad is here!"
   But it was Hare. "That's not my dad!" cried Patty.
   "Lost your dad?" Hare said, as the snow fell more thickly.
"He's down there. You'll miss him unless you go quickly!"
   Patty leaped headlong and rolled round and round...
to the end of the slope – and guess what she found?
   "There he is!" Patty grinned. "That's Dad right there."
And she waved to her dad through the cold snowy air.
   But it wasn't him. "That's not my dad!" cried Patty.

"Lost your dad?" Puffin smiled,
seeing Patty's dismay.
"He made you this snow
bear to show you the way."
A little while later, a deep
rumbling sound...
was echoing out from
a den in the ground.
Then Puffin, Walrus,
Seal, Whale, Fox
and Hare... all smiled at the
snores coming out of that lair...

"THAT'S MY DAD!" cried Patty.
And she was right. It was!

Soon Patty and Dad were together again...
cosy and warm in their underground den!

The Ungrateful Tiger

Once there was a village that was plagued by tigers, so that the children couldn't play outside and the people were afraid to leave their homes. At last the villagers had had enough, and they dug a deep pit to trap the beasts.

One day, a man was on his way to visit the village when he heard a growl coming from below the ground. The man walked toward the noise and found a tiger stuck in the pit.

"What are you doing down there?" the man asked the tiger.

"I'm stuck," the tiger replied. "I was walking along minding my own business when I fell into this hole, and now I can't get out again. I'm so hungry and thirsty! Please help me."

"But if I help you to get out, you might eat me," the man replied. "After all, you did say you were hungry."

"I wouldn't do that because I would be so grateful," the tiger assured him.

The man hated to see animals suffering, so he got a tree branch and used it to help pull the tiger out of the hole.

When the tiger was safely out of the hole the man continued on his way.

Suddenly, he felt the tiger's hot breath on his neck.

"What are you doing?" cried the man.

"I am going to eat you!" the tiger replied.

"But that's not f-f-fair," the man stammered. "You said you would be grateful!"

"I am," the tiger replied. "But humans dug that trap, and you are a human, so I am going to eat you."

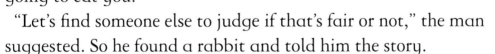

"Let's find someone else to judge if that's fair or not," the man suggested. So he found a rabbit and told him the story.

"I think you had better show me what happened," said the rabbit. So they all went back to the hole in the ground.

"Show the rabbit exactly where you were," the man told the tiger. So the tiger jumped into the pit once again.

"Repeat what you said," said the man. And the tiger did.

The rabbit listened carefully. "In my opinion, it is not fair for you to eat this man," he said, when the tiger had finished. "He did not dig the hole! You should be grateful for his help."

"All right," agreed the tiger. "I promise not to eat him. Now will you help me out of this hole?"

But the rabbit and the man shook their heads, for how could they know if the tiger was telling the truth?

Cocks Crow

Cocks crow in the morn,
To tell us to rise.
And he who sleeps late,
Will never be wise.
For early to bed,
And early to rise,
Is the way to be healthy,
wealthy and wise.

Buzz and Hum

Buzz says the blue fly,
Hum says the bee,
Buzz and hum they say...
And so do we.

Can You Walk on Tiptoe?

Can you walk on tiptoe,
As softly as a cat?
And can you slink along the road,
Softly, just like that?
Can you take great big strides,
Like an ostrich can?
Or walk along so slowly,
Just like a bent old man?

Frog Went a-Courtin'

Frog went a-courtin' an' he did ride,
A bunch of roses by his side.
He rode up to Miss Mousie's door,
Gave a loud knock and gave a loud call.
He said, "Miss Mousie, are you in?"
"Yes, kind sir, I sit and spin."
He took Miss Mousie on his knee,
And said, "Miss Mousie, will you marry me?"

Sparrow Got Up Early

Sparrow got up early,
At the break of day,
And went to Jenny's window,
To sing a roundelay.
He sang a song of love
To pretty Jenny Wren,
And when he got unto the end,
Then he began again.

Dame Trot and Her Cat

When Dame Trot had her dinner
Kitty would wait,
And was sure to receive
A treat from her plate.

The Clumsy Hippo

Grace the Hippo was having a lovely time wallowing in the waters of Lake Haha, when the flamingos came wading by. They looked so beautiful that Grace rolled onto her back to get a better look.

"Tut, tut!" they squawked as Grace showered them with cold water.

"Sorry," said Grace, hanging her head. She was so embarrassed that she heaved herself out of the water and waddled away. "I wish I could move gracefully like the flamingos," she thought. "I'm just so clumsy. I can't imagine why Mum and Dad called me Grace!"

Grace walked sadly along the riverbank. She didn't see Crocodile lounging in the sun until it was too late.

"Ouch!" cried Crocodile, as Grace trod on his tail. "Watch where you stomp those great big feet."

"Sorry," said Grace, blushing.

Grace went to eat some grass. She tore up a great hunk and began to chomp on it noisily. She chewed the grass round and round, licked her enormous teeth, and burped!

"Really!" said Zebra, who was grazing nearby. "Didn't your parents teach you any manners?'

"Sorry," said Grace. "It just popped out!"

Grace decided to go for a run. She might be a little on the round side, but she enjoyed running. She was having a great time until Meerkat stuck his head out of a burrow.

"Hey, clumsy!" he bellowed. "Do you mind? Your footsteps are shaking my home."

"I beg your pardon," said Grace.

Grace plonked herself beneath her favourite Acacia tree to think. She didn't notice that Anteater was already sitting there until she heard a yell.

"Ouch!" he shrieked. "Get your big bottom off my head."

"Oops! Sorry," said Grace. "I'm so clumsy, I think I'd better keep out of everyone's way today."

She waded sadly back into Lake Haha, dived beneath the surface, and paddled along. Soon she was gliding swiftly through the water. The fish waved happily to her. Then Turtle came and joined her in a game of chase. Suddenly Grace smiled. Now she remembered why Mum and Dad had called her Grace. When she was swimming, she wasn't clumsy at all. In fact, she was really rather 'graceful'.

Four Little Birds

Four little birds all huddled together.
The first one said,
"My, what cold weather."
The second one said,
"The sky is getting grey."
The third one said,
"Let's fly away."
The fourth little bird
Never opened his mouth.
So they all flew away
To the sunny south.

Poor Dog Bright

Poor Dog Bright
Ran away with all his might,
Because the cat was after him –
Poor Dog Bright!

Poor Cat Fright
Ran away with all her might,
Because the dog was after her –
Poor Cat Fright!

The Bumble Bee!

The bumble bee is small and round,
It flies about above the ground,
With stripes of yellow on its back,
Or maybe it has stripes of black!
Two little wings to help it zoom,
So it can go from bloom to bloom,
Collecting pollen on its feet,
To make some honey, sweet to eat.
But whatever else it does,
The noise it makes is...
Buzz! Buzz! Buzz!

The Cuckoo's a Fine Bird

The cuckoo's a fine bird,
She sings as she flies,
She brings us good tidings,
She tells us no lies.

She lays her eggs
In another bird's nest,
And then she sings "Cuckoo!"
And flies off to rest.

Mowgli and Baloo's Lessons

One day Bagheera, the black panther, was watching Baloo, the big brown bear, teach Mowgli the Law of the Jungle. There was so much to learn that Mowgli started getting things wrong and Baloo cuffed him softly around the ears. Mowgli was so cross that he hid in the trees.

"He's so small," said the black panther. "How can you expect him to learn so much?"

"A man cub is a man cub, and he must learn all the Law of the Jungle," replied Baloo. "Nothing is too small to be killed. That's why I hit him, very softly."

"Softly, indeed, old Iron Fist," grunted Bagheera.

"Better he gets the odd pat from me than come to harm through ignorance," replied Baloo.

"At the moment I'm teaching him the **Master Words of the Jungle** to protect him from all the jungle creatures. I'll call him and he will say them. Come, Little Brother."

Mowgli slid down a tree trunk.

"My head is ringing," the boy complained, looking annoyed.

"I come for Bagheera, not you, Baloo!"

Baloo was a little upset by this because he loved Mowgli.

"Man cub, why don't you tell Bagheera the 'Master Words of the Jungle'," said Baloo.

"Master Words for which people?" said Mowgli, who was delighted to show off. "The jungle has many tongues."

Then he rattled through the Words of the Animals, the Birds and the Snakes. When he had finished he clapped his hands and made horrible faces at Baloo.

"One day I'll lead my own tribe through the branches. We'll throw branches and dirt at old Baloo," sang Mowgli.

"Mowgli," growled Baloo. "You've been talking with the Monkey People. They're evil."

Mowgli looked at Bagheera to see if the panther was angry, too, and Bagheera's face looked like cold ice.

"When you hurt my head, they came down and gave me nuts and said I should be their leader. No one else cared," he sniffed.

"They have no leader! They lie," said Bagheera.

"Well, I like them. They play all day," pouted Mowgli.

"Listen," said the bear, and his voice rumbled like thunder. "They have no Law. They creep around and spy. They boast and chatter and pretend to be great when they are not. We of the jungle ignore them even if they throw dirt at our heads."

As he spoke, a shower of nuts and twigs rained down.

The evil Monkey People shrieked above. One of them had had a brilliant idea. He'd decided that Mowgli would be a useful person to have in their tribe. He could teach them how to make huts like the ones humans lived in. With Mowgli's help, they would become the wisest people in the jungle.

The Monkey People waited until Baloo, Bagheera and Mowgli were asleep, then they grabbed the little boy and swung him through the treetops.

Mowgli felt sick and giddy as they bounded, crashed and whooped from one tree to the next. He knew that he had to get word back to his friends, for at the speed they were going Baloo and Bagheera would never be able to keep up. Mowgli saw Chil, the kite bird, circling above and remembered Baloo's lessons.

"We be of one blood, you and I. Tell Baloo and Bagheera that Mowgli passed this way."

Meanwhile, Baloo and Bagheera, who had heard Mowgli's cries, followed below. Before long, they came across Kaa, the python.

"What are you hunting?" hissed the snake.

"Monkey People, who have snatched Mowgli," explained Baloo.

"I'll help you hunt them," hissed Kaa.

Just then, there was a shout from above. It was Chil, the kite.

"The Monkey People have taken him to their ruined city."

"Come," said Bagheera. "We must go there at once."
And off they all raced.

Meanwhile, the monkeys had gathered around Mowgli, chattering about how wonderful they were. Mowgli began to think that they were all mad. He was wondering how he could escape when Bagheera raced down the hill and began knocking monkeys left and right. But there were too many, and soon the brave panther was fighting for his life.

"Roll to the water tank," cried Mowgli. "They won't follow."

With a burst of strength, Bagheera threw off his attackers and lunged into the water tank. Just at that moment, Baloo lumbered in and took up the fight. Then Kaa pounced, eager and ready to kill.

Kaa was everything the monkeys feared. With one hiss, the monkeys scattered with cries of "It is Kaa, run, run!"

Mowgli was free from the Monkey People's clutches.

And after that day, he always tried his best to remember everything Baloo taught him.

The Octopus

The arms on the octopus number eight:
One, two, three, four, five, six, seven, eight!
All curled up, then pointing straight,
One, two, three, four, five, six, seven, eight!
In the ocean, octopuses wait,
One, two, three, four, five, six, seven, eight,
For clams and crabs to put on their plate!

I Wish I Were a Fish

How I wish I were a fish!
My day would begin,
Flapping my fins.
I'd make a commotion,
Out in the ocean.
It would be cool
To swim in a school.
In the sea,
I'd move so free,
With just one thought:
Don't get caught!

Oysters

Oysters are creatures
Without any features.

Ten White Seagulls

Ten white seagulls, just see them fly.
Over the mountain, and up to the sky.
Ten white seagulls crying aloud,
Spread out their wings, and fly over a cloud.
Ten white seagulls on a bright day.
Pretty white seagulls, fly, fly away!

Whale Song

Who can fail
To spot the whale?
She's as big as a mountain,
And spouts like a fountain.

The Penguin

The penguin's a bird that cannot fly,
But swims like a torpedo,
And on the ice it looks so nice
Dressed in its own tuxedo!

Little Penguin and Friends

Little Penguin had no one
to play with.

"Why don't you build
a snow den?" suggested
Mummy Penguin.

So Little Penguin used his
tiny wings to scoop up as
much snow as he could into
a pile. It was hard work on his own,

but he kept on until he had made a giant fluffy, white mound
of snow.

He was very tired by now, though, and he was just about to
give up when Little Polar Bear came wandering by.

"What are you doing?" Little Polar Bear asked his friend,
curiously.

"I'm trying to build a snow den," replied Little Penguin. "But
my flippers are very small, and I'm getting very tired."

"Can I help?" asked Little Polar Bear. "My paws
are good for digging in the snow."

So Little Polar Bear began to dig with his big furry paws, and
Little Penguin helped. It was hard work, but they kept on

until they had made a big
snowy cave.

Little Seal came by.

"That looks like fun,"
he said. "Do you need
any help? My fins and
tail are perfect for
patting down snow."

So Little Seal patted
the snow den to make it smooth and shiny, while Little
Penguin and Polar Bear helped. It was hard work, but they
kept on patting until the den gleamed.

Little Fox Pup scampered over to admire their work.

"Shall I use my tail to sweep away the snow?" he offered.
And he swished his tail back and forth to clear a path.

At last Little Penguin's snow
den was finished.

"What shall we do now?"
asked his new friends.

"Play in the snow den,
of course!" laughed
Little Penguin excitedly.
"It's just the
right size for
four friends!"

No One Like You

Ruff was hungry.
A huge grumble
rumbled around
his tummy. He
could hear Mum
in the kitchen,
and a delicious
smell of freshly baked
cupcakes sailed past his nose.

"Yummy," thought Ruff. At first, Ruff
skipped into the kitchen – Mum was tidying up.

"Would you like some help?" asked Ruff. "I could try one of
those cupcakes for you."

"Oh, really," said Mum smiling.

"No one makes cakes like you," said Ruff.

Ruff was bored. He twiddled his fingers, tapped his toes, and
twiddled his fingers again. He had no one to play with.

Later, Ruff tiptoed back into the living room – Mum
was reading.

"Would you like something better to read?" asked Ruff.
"I could find you an exciting story."

"Oh, really," said Mum smiling.

"No one tells a story like you," said Ruff.

Ruff was annoyed. He was trying to make a model car,
but he couldn't put it together. Then he had an idea!

He galloped into the garden – Mum was digging.

"Would you like something fun to do?" asked Ruff. "I could let you help me with my model."

"Oh, really," said Mum smiling.

"No one is as much fun as you," said Ruff.

It was bedtime! Mum tucked Ruff into bed.

Ruff was feeling scared. He didn't like the shadows that flickered all around – it was very quiet. Then he had an idea.

Ruff crept out of his bedroom and into Mum's to wake Mum.

"Would you like someone to cuddle?" asked Ruff. "I'm very good at cuddling."

"Oh, really," said Mum smiling.

"No one cuddles like you," yawned Ruff, climbing into Mum's bed.

"Oh, really," said Mum… "Well, no one loves you as much as I do. Because there is **no one like you!**"

The Lemur Dance

Louis the Lemur had a secret. He loved to dance, but none
of the other lemurs knew, because Louis was very shy.
He never went down to the river to play. He never joined
in games of hide-and-seek. And when all the other lemurs
decided to do a Lemur Dance, Louis would run away and hide.

One day, when the other lemurs were playing in the forest,
Louis crept out from his hiding place and began to sway.
He closed his eyes and began to twirl. He hummed, and then
leaped into the air and spun around and around. He was
having such a wonderful time that he didn't hear the other
lemurs coming back. When he opened his eyes and saw them,
he stopped dancing at once!

"Don't stop!" cried Melanie the Lemur, grabbing his paw.
"You're a great dancer!"

"Wow," thought Louis, as they twirled around and
around. "Dancing with other lemurs isn't at all
scary. It's even better than
dancing alone!"

After that,
Louis always
played and
danced with the
other lemurs. And
he was never ever
shy ever again.

SSSSHHH!

One morning Lion was very tired, so he curled up for a nap.
He was just dozing off when Monkey began to screech.
"Ssssh!" roared Lion angrily. "Can't a lion get any peace?"
Monkey crept away.

Lion settled back down and closed his eyes. He was just
beginning to snore when Elephant came stomping by.
"Ssssh!" roared Lion angrily. "Can't a lion get any peace?"
"Sorry," whispered Elephant, and he tiptoed away.

Suddenly there was a loud hiss. It was Snake passing by.
"Ssssh!" roared Lion angrily. "Can't a lion get any peace?"
"S…s…sorry," hissed Snake.

Lion closed his eyes again, but it was no use. No matter how
hard he tried, he was much too angry by now to fall asleep.

"What you need is a jungle lullaby," squeaked a little mouse.
"Listen to the whispering breeze, and the stream bubbling
down to the waterhole. Listen to the crickets singing in the
grass. That's a jungle lullaby! Can you hear it?"

But Lion never said a word. He was fast asleep. Ssssh!

Little Dolphin

Little Dolphin was a friendly creature who loved to visit all his ocean friends. But sometimes when he visited them it made him feel just a little bit sad.

"They are all so talented," he said to himself. "And I'm just a boring old dolphin. I wish I was more like them."

One morning, Little Dolphin met his friends for a play by the seashore. As usual, he couldn't help admiring everyone. Octopus was amazing. He could juggle urchins and tickle fish at the same time. He could even pick up seaweed with seven tentacles, while he shook hands with the eighth.

"I wish I had tentacles like you, Octopus," sighed Little Dolphin. "Then I could do lots of things at once."

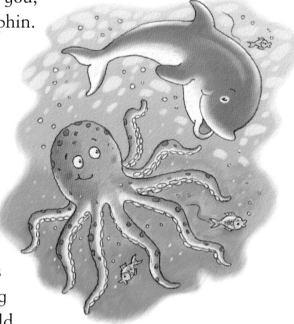

Octopus blushed and told Dolphin not to be silly.

"But silly is exactly what I am," thought Little Dolphin sadly. He turned around to watch Crab.

Crab had two gigantic claws for grabbing, and lots of smaller claws for scuttling around on the sand. He could even scuttle across the seabed sideways.

"I wish I had claws like you, Crab," sighed Little Dolphin, looking at them enviously.

"Well, I don't have claws either," said Turtle, trying to make Little Dolphin feel better.

"No," said Little Dolphin. "But you do have flippers, so you can soar through the water. I can't do anything special!"

"What do you mean?" cried Turtle in surprise.

"Of course you can," added Octopus. "No one in the whole ocean can leap and do tricks like you."

Little Dolphin thought for a moment, then a smile began to spread across his face.

"You're right," he cried, leaping out of the water and performing a perfect somersault right in front of all his friends.

"Maybe being a little dolphin isn't so bad, after all," he said. "Come on everyone! Let's play!"

And that's exactly what they all did.

The Egg

Baby Parrot lived in a nest with Mummy and a big white egg.

"I'm going to find some food," said Mummy one day.
"You must look after **the egg** until I return."

Baby Parrot watched **the egg** for a very long time.
She moved it around to make sure it was comfortable.
She wrapped her wings around it to make sure it was warm.
Then she gave it a kiss. "I'm very good at looking after eggs,"
she squawked, as she watched a pretty butterfly fly by.

Just then, she heard the monkeys playing in the trees.
Baby Parrot tried to call like a monkey, too. She peered over
the edge of the nest and laughed at their games.

Suddenly Baby Parrot remembered **the egg**. She looked
around and gulped. It was broken. Mummy would be furious!

But when she returned, Mummy wasn't angry at all.

"Don't worry," she said, as a little parrot popped out of the
broken eggshell. **"The egg** has hatched while I was away.
Now you've got a new baby sister to play with!"

Stinky the Skunk

Stinky was a little skunk who didn't like her name.
It made her feel ridiculous and often blush with shame.
It didn't even suit her, because she didn't smell…
She always washed her paws and fur, and her tail as well.
"I wish my name was Dancer, Rose or even Fleur…
Or maybe Stripy would be nice, to match my stripy fur."
Her mother smiled kindly. "From now I'll call you Rose."
But as these words were spoken she wrinkled up her nose.
Rose was so excited… she'd lifted up her tail,
And sprayed a stinky, skunky scent – all along the trail.
Rose giggled loudly and said, "I must admit,
When I am excited I do stink just a bit!"

The Swimming Lesson

Baby Seal was very excited. Today his family was taking him for his first swimming lesson. Baby Seal watched as the others slipped into the ocean. **Plop! Plop! Plop!**

"Don't worry," called his sister. "It's lovely. Jump in."

"No thanks," said Baby Seal, and he slid away across the ice.

"Dip a flipper," called Mum.

"Dangle your tail," said his sister.

"Dive in," suggested Dad.

Baby Seal closed his eyes and hummed so that he couldn't hear. Swimming looked much too scary. He was so busy humming that he didn't hear the ice cracking.

"Help!" wailed Baby Seal as he crashed through the ice and sank under the water.

Quick as a flash, he wiggled his flippers and tail. Then, much to his surprise, he found himself bobbing up by Mum.

"You're swimming," smiled Mum.

"Yes, I am," laughed Baby Seal, twizzling in delight. Then he dived under the water with a flip of his tail to chase after his sister. "Swimming's easy when you know how!" he cried.

Mouse's New Home

It was midwinter, and Mouse was searching for a cosy, new indoor home. He crept into the farmhouse and looked around until he found an old cobweb in the pantry.

"This will make a lovely hammock," he thought, as he climbed in and snuggled down. But the cobweb broke, and Mouse fell to the ground with a thud!

Next, Mouse spotted a slipper by the back door. "That's just the right shape for a bed," he decided. So he crawled inside and curled up. But just as he was falling asleep, the farmer's wife came home and pushed her foot into the slipper.

"Ouch!" squeaked Mouse, scampering off into the kitchen.

There by the fire was a soft, furry cushion.

"That's more like it," thought Mouse, and he climbed up. Suddenly there was a loud HISS. It wasn't a cushion at all. It was Spike, the farm cat!

"Eeeeeeeeek," cried Mouse, darting into a hole in the wall to hide. He waited quietly until Spike was gone. And then he looked around. The hole was small, warm and very cosy.

"Ooooooooohh!" smiled Mouse happily. "This really will make the perfect home!"

The Crow
and the Pitcher

One hot summer day, when there had been no rain for months
and all the ponds and rivers had dried up, a thirsty crow was
searching for a drink. At last he spotted a pitcher of cool water
in a garden, and flew down to take a drink. But when
he put his head into the neck of the pitcher, it was only half
full, and the crow could not reach the water.

Now, the crow was a smart bird, so he came up with a plan —
he would break the neck of the pitcher, then reach down to the
water below.

Tap! Tap! Tap! The crow pecked the pitcher with his
sharp beak again and again, but it was so hard and strong,
he couldn't make even the tiniest crack.

The crow did not give up easily, so he thought of another plan. He would tip the pitcher over. The bird pushed and pushed as hard as he could, but the pitcher was very heavy, and it would not move at all.

The poor crow knew that if he did not get a drink soon he would die of thirst. He had to find some way of getting to the water in the pitcher! As he looked around, wondering what to do, he saw some pebbles on the path, and he had an idea.

He picked up a pebble in his beak and dropped it into the pitcher. The water level rose a little. The bird got another pebble and dropped it in. The water rose a little more. The crow worked very hard, dropping more and more pebbles into the pitcher until the water was almost at the top.

At last the bird was able to reach the water – and he drank and drank until he could drink no more. His clever idea had saved his life.

Aesop's moral:
Little by little
does the trick.

Kitty Cat Mole

Kitty Cat Mole,
Jumped over a coal,
And in her best petticoat
Burned a great hole.
She'll have no more milk,
Until her best petticoat's
Mended with silk.

I Had a Little Horse

I had a little horse,
His name was Dapple Grey,
His head was made of gingerbread,
His tail was made of hay.

Can You See a Rabbit?

Can you see a rabbit,
With two ears so very long,
Watch him hop, hop, hop about,
On legs so small and strong.
He nibbles, nibbles carrots,
For his dinner every day;
As soon as he has had enough
He scampers fast away!

Slippery Snake

Oh, I wish I was a slippery snake,
Oh, I wish I was a slippery snake,
Oh, I'd slither across the floor
And slip under the door,
Oh, I wish I was a slippery snake.

All Around the Barnyard

All around the barnyard
The animals are fast asleep.
Sleeping cows and horses,
Sleeping pigs and sheep.
Here comes the cocky rooster
To sound his daily alarm.
Cock-a-doodle-doo!
Wake up, sleepy farm!

Jenny Wren

As little Jenny Wren
Was sitting by the shed,
She waggled with her tail,
And nodded with her head.

You're Not My Mum!

Gerry and Mum were walking
one day, when a line of termites
came marching their way.

Gerry watched as they
passed by, one by one...
but when he looked up
his Mummy was gone!

"Lost your mum?" asked
Sunbird. "She's nearby, don't you
worry! The termites will show you
the way if you hurry."

So off Gerry galloped in great leaps and bounds,
till he screeched to a halt by some huge termite mounds.

"Aha!" Gerry cried. "Now I'm on the right trail.
That looks like my mum's tufty tail!"

But it was Elephant.

"**You're not my mum!**" Gerry cried.

"Lost your mum?" smiled Elephant. "Just let me think.
Is she down at the riverside having a drink?"

Gerry ran to the river as quick as a flash.
There he saw something blinking and heard a loud splash.

"Aha!" Gerry cried. "Now what's that I spy?
That sounds like Mum drinking – and look, there's her eye!"

But it was Crocodile.

"**You're not my mum!**" he cried.

"Lost your mum?" cackled Croc. "Take a look over there.
I'm sure I saw something with spotty brown hair."

A little way off, Gerry heard a strange sound –
something was snoring nearby on the ground!

"Aha!" Gerry cried, as he peered through a gap.
"I'm sure that's my mum! She's just taking a nap!"

But it was Leopard.

"**You're not my mum!**" cried Gerry.

Leopard yawned as he woke. "There's one place you could try.

In that baobab tree I heard something up high."
  Near the baobab tree Gerry started to stare.
Was there something familiar moving up there?
  "Aha!" Gerry cried. "That looks just like Mum's neck,
stretching up for some leaves. I'll just go and check!"
  But it was Snake.

"You're not my mum!" cried Gerry.
  "Lossst your mum?" whispered Snake. "If she loves to chew,
there are nice tasssty leaves in that clump of bamboo."
  By now Gerry felt like he'd been searching for hours.
But at last – what was standing behind those bright flowers?
  "Aha!" Gerry cried, and he started to laugh.
"Who else could have feet like that but a giraffe?"
  But it was Zebra.
"You're not my mum!" cried Gerry.
  "Lost your mum?" chuckled Zebra, as he flicked off the flies.

"Go back to the woods, and you'll get a surprise."
As Gerry came close to the thick jungle glade,
he saw some giraffes in the cool of the shade.
Then from the trees came a voice, saying...
"Hi, little guy!"
Gerry looked up and cried...
"That's my mum!"
So Gerry and Mum,
in the shade of a tree,
had a big Mummy hug
that was snug as can be.

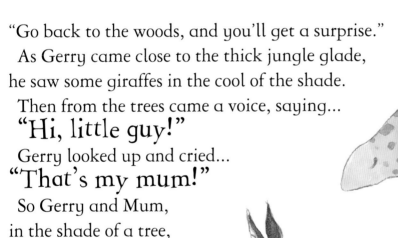

The Fox and the Goat

One hot day, a thirsty fox was searching for something to drink. At last he found a well in a farmyard. He stuck his nose over the edge, but the water was too far down. Very carefully, he balanced on the side, trying to reach the cool, clear water. But though his nose was so close that he could smell it, he still couldn't quite reach the water.

The fox made one last try, stretching out his tongue with all his might. SPLASH! he toppled right in.

The sides of the well were so slippery that when the fox tried to climb out, he just kept sliding back down. He was stuck!

After a while, a goat came by looking for a drink. He was surprised to see the fox in the water.

"What on earth are you doing down there?" he asked.

"Just cooling down," replied the fox. "The water in this well is the best for miles around. Why don't you jump in and try it."

The goat was very hot and thirsty, and the water did look very refreshing, so he jumped in to join the fox.

"You're right!" said the goat, taking a long drink and relaxing in the water. "It's lovely and cool down here."

Soon the goat decided that it was time to go on his way.

"How do we get out?" he asked.

"That is a bit of a problem," the fox admitted. "But I've got an idea. If you stick your legs out, you can wedge yourself in the well. Then I can climb on your back and jump out."

"That's all very well, but what about me?" the goat bleated.

"Once I've climbed out, I can help you get out," the fox explained.

So the goat wedged himself against the walls of the well and the fox clambered onto his back and leaped out.

"Thank you," laughed the fox, as he turned to leave.

"Hold on! What about me? How am I going to get out?" cried the goat.

"You should have thought about that before you jumped in," replied the sly fox — and off he ran.

Aesop's moral: Look before you leap.

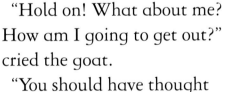

Wiggly Woo

There's a worm at the bottom of the garden,
And his name is Wiggly Woo.
There's a worm at the bottom of the garden,
And all that he can do,
Is wiggle all night
And wiggle all day,
Whatever else the people do say,
There's a worm at the bottom of the garden,
And his name is Wiggly Woo!

Ding, Dong, Bell

Ding, dong, bell,
Kitty's in the well!
Who put her in?
Little Tommy Green.
Who pulled her out?
Little Johnny Stout.
What a naughty boy was that
To try to hurt poor kitty cat,
Who never did any harm,
But chased the mice in his father's barn.

The Tortoise and the Eagle

There was once a tortoise who was very unhappy with his life. He hated crawling around on the ground all the time, and was very jealous of the birds who could soar high into the sky. He was sure that if he could just get up into the air, he would be able to fly as well as they could.

One day, the tortoise was sitting on a rock by the seashore, when an eagle flew down and landed nearby.

"Will you teach me how to fly?" the tortoise asked the eagle.

"Don't be so silly," said the eagle. "How could you fly? You don't have any wings."

"I'm sure I could fly, if I could just get off the ground," the tortoise insisted. "You are a big, strong bird. You could carry me into the sky, and once I'm up there, you could tell me what to do and let me go. Then I could fly away."

"Listen," the eagle explained, "I have been flying around

in the sky for many years, and the only creatures I have ever seen up there all have one thing in common: they have wings!"

But the tortoise wouldn't give up. "I will give you all the treasures in the ocean if you will teach me to fly," he promised the eagle.

Finally, the eagle got tired of listening to the tortoise begging and pleading.

"All right," he agreed. "I will take you up into the sky, and when we get there, I will let you go and you can try to fly."

The tortoise was delighted that he would be leaving the ground at last.

The eagle carried him right out over the sea. They were so high that the tortoise could almost touch the clouds.

"Are you ready?" the eagle said. "Stretch out your legs and flap them."

"Yes, yes, let me go," the tortoise cried impatiently.

So the eagle let go of the tortoise, who stretched out his legs and flapped them furiously, as he had been told.

Can you guess what happened next? The tortoise dropped like a stone, and fell... down, down, down, into the sea.

Aesop's moral: Demanding your own way can backfire.

Little Bo-Peep

Little Bo-Peep has lost her sheep,
And doesn't know where to find them;
Leave them alone,
And they'll come home,
Bringing their tails behind them.

Five Little Chickens

Said the first little chicken, with a queer little squirm,
"I wish I could find a fat little worm."
Said the next little chicken, with an odd little shrug,
"I wish I could find a fat little slug."
Said the third little chicken, with a sharp little squeal,
"I wish I could find some nice yellow meal."
Said the fourth little chicken, with a small sigh of grief,
"I wish I could find a little green leaf."
Said the fifth little chicken, with a faint little moan,
"I wish I could find a wee gravel stone."
"Now see here," said the mother, from the green garden patch,
"If you want your breakfast, just come here and scratch."

A Funny Bird

The turkey is a funny bird,
Its head goes bobble-bobble;
And all he knows is just one word...
And that is gobble, gobble!

Milking Time

How come a cow never says ow!
Whenever there's milking to do?
It doesn't say ow!
For it pleases the cow,
So instead, the cow says moo!

Two Little Kittens

Two little kittens, one stormy night,
Began to quarrel and then to fight.
One had a mouse and the other had none,
And that's the way the quarrel was begun.

Cock-a-doodle-choo!

The farm is in a flurry.
The rooster's caught the flu.
His cock-a-doodle-doo
Has changed to cock-a-doodle-choo!

Kitty White

Kitty White so slyly comes,
To catch the Mousie Grey;
But Mousie hears her softly creep,
And quickly runs away!

Big Paws

Big paws, big black nose,
Stubby tail, and growl he goes.
What is he? Well, who knows?
He sleeps all winter
When it snows.

Six Swans

Once upon a time a king was tricked by an evil old witch into marrying her daughter. Now, the king had been married before, and had six sons and a beautiful daughter of his own, whom he loved very much. The king was afraid that the new queen would harm his children, so he hid them in a faraway castle. Even the king didn't know the way there. He had to roll a ball of magic string through the forest to show him the path.

The king secretly visited his children every evening. The new queen soon began to wonder where the king went each night. So she tricked one of the king's servants into telling her the secret. When she heard about the children, she knew she had to find them.

The very next day the queen searched the castle until she found the ball of magic string. Then, using a spell, she made some magic shirts of white silk.

When the king went hunting the next day, the queen took the magic ball of string and the shirts she had made and went to the hidden castle. As soon as the queen saw the six sons, she took out the magic shirts and quickly threw them over their heads. In a flash, they turned into swans and flew away.

When the sister returned home and found her brothers gone, she went in search of them. She wandered for many days until she came across a hunting lodge. Inside were six little beds. Suddenly, the girl heard the beating of wings, so she hid beneath one of the

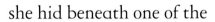

beds. Six white swans flew in through the window and landed on the beds. The swans blew on one another and the girl gasped with amazement. Their feathers fell off to reveal that they weren't swans, but boys.

"My brothers!" she cried.

The boys were overjoyed to see their sister. But they were also worried.

"You can't stay here," they said. "It's a robbers' den. If they find you, they will be angry. Each day, we are human for just fifteen minutes before we turn into swans again."

"How can I free you from the spell?" asked their sister.
"It is too much to ask. You must sew six shirts from nettles," said one brother. "And you must not utter a word for six years."

"I will do it," cried the sister.
And with that, her brothers turned back into swans again.

The princess went out and began picking nettles at once.

She did not mind that they stung her soft fingers. She simply sat under a tree and began to sew.

Before long, a king from another kingdom rode by.

"What are you doing?" he asked.

Of course, the girl could not speak. She just kept on sewing, trying not to flinch as the nettles stung her hands.

The king fell in love on the spot. He took the girl home and married her. But still the girl would not speak, and every day she insisted on sewing her nettle shirts.

The king's mother was jealous of the new queen and wanted to get rid of her. When the girl had her first baby, the king's mother stole the child and gave it to a woodcutter. She told everyone the queen had given the baby away.

Of course, the queen would not speak to defend herself. She just kept on sewing. Luckily, the king did not believe his mother.

A year later, the queen had another baby, and once again the king's mother gave the child to the woodcutter.

"Now do you believe me?" she asked of the king.

The king shook his head.

But when their third child disappeared, the king began to have doubts.

"She only wants to sew all day," he thought. "Maybe Mother speaks the truth."

The king begged his wife to defend herself, but she would not. Sadly, the king decided she was guilty.

"You will be punished in the morning," he announced.

The queen sewed all night. It was the last night of the six years she had been given to complete the nettle shirts.

At sunrise, the six shirts were almost finished. Only one sleeve was missing. When the king came for the queen, the six white swans appeared out of thin air. The queen threw the nettle shirts over their heads. At once, the swans turned into boys – though the youngest had a wing instead of an arm.

"At last I can speak," cried the girl. She quickly told the king about her brothers, and how his own mother had given their children to the woodcutter.

When the king heard the truth, he sent his mother away and went to rescue his children, from the woodcutter.

After that, the king, queen, their children and the six brothers lived happily ever after.

I Had a Poodle

I had a little poodle,
His coat was silver grey,
One day I thought I'd bathe him,
To wash the dirt away.
I washed my little poodle,
Then dried him with a towel.
My poodle seemed to like his bath!
He didn't even growl.

Two Little Puppies

Two little puppy dogs
Lying in a heap,
Soft and woolly
And fast asleep.
Along came a kitty cat,
Creeping near...
"Meow!" she cried,
Right in their ear.
Two little puppy dogs
After one kitty cat,
Did you ever play tag like that?

Welcome to the Jungle

Jasper the monkey lived deep in the jungle with his mum, dad and lots of uncles and aunts. When Jasper wasn't busy playing with the other monkeys, he loved exploring the jungle and making new friends.

One day something very exciting happened. Jasper's mum gave birth to a baby boy, called Charlie. Jasper was very excited. He couldn't wait to show his new brother the jungle and introduce him to all his old friends.

"Can I take Charlie exploring?" Jasper asked his mum.

"As long as you take good care of him, replied Mum. "And you'll have to carry him – he's much too small to walk very far."

"No problem," laughed Jasper. And he picked up Charlie and began to carry him through the jungle. They had only got as far as the river when Jasper began to puff and pant. Charlie wriggled and screeched with glee. Jasper panted even harder. Charlie was heavier than he'd thought.

"Oh, dear," sighed Jasper. "I don't think I'm going to be able to carry you very far, after all. I think we'll have to go home."

Jasper put Charlie down and sat down on the riverbank.
Jasper felt very sad. He had been looking forward to
introducing Charlie to all his friends. As he stared into the
river, a pair of eyes and two nostrils popped out of the water.
Then a crocodile with huge teeth rose to the surface.

Charlie jumped back in fright.

"Don't worry," laughed Jasper. "It's only Cressida the
Crocodile." He turned to the crocodile and smiled.

"Hi, Cressida," he called. "Come and meet Charlie, my baby
brother. I was going to take him around the jungle to meet
everyone, but he's too heavy to carry."

"I could give you a lift," suggested Cressida.
"Jump on my back
and I'll take you
on a river ride."

"What a great
idea," said Jasper.
The brothers
jumped onto the
crocodile's back and
were soon gliding
through the jungle.
Jasper had a wonderful
time introducing Charlie to his

old friends, and just as much fun making new friends along the
way. But both Jasper and Charlie agreed that Cressida was...
the best friend of all!

A Boy's Song

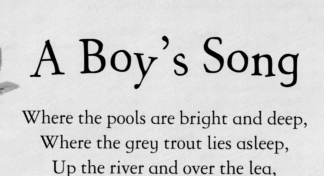

Where the pools are bright and deep,
Where the grey trout lies asleep,
Up the river and over the lea,
That's the way for my dog and me.

Where the blackbird sings the latest,
Where the hawthorn blooms the sweetest,
Where the nestlings chirp and flee,
That's the way for my dog and me.

Where the mowers mow the cleanest,
Where the hay lies thick and greenest,
There to track the homeward bee,
That's the way for my dog and me.

Where the hazel bank is steepest,
Where the shadow falls the deepest,
Where the clustering nuts fall free,
That's the way for my dog and me.

Why the boys should drive away
Little sweet maidens from the play,
Or love to banter and fight so well,
That's the thing I never could tell.

But this I know, I love to play
Through the meadow, among the hay;
Up the water and over the lea,
That's the way for my dog and me.

The Town Mouse and the Country Mouse

Once a town mouse went to visit his cousin in the country. The country mouse was very pleased to see his relative and made him as welcome as he could. Although he only had simple food in his pantry, he offered his cousin everything that he had: peas, barley, nuts and cheese.

The town mouse picked at the food, while his country cousin made do with a piece of barley straw.

"I don't know how you can put up with such boring food," the town mouse said after dinner. "Your life here is so dull. It's much more fun in town. We have streets full of carriages and smartly dressed people, and wonderful food for the taking. Why don't you come and see?"

So the country mouse packed a bag and the cousins set off.

It was dark by the time they arrived in town, and the country mouse was dazzled by the bright city lights. At last, the two mice crept into the house where the town mouse lived.

The country mouse stared in wonder at the velvet chairs

and fine furniture. On the dining table lay the remains of a banquet. After offering his cousin a seat, the town mouse ran back and forth bringing delicacies for his cousin to try — lobster, venison with red wine sauce and finally (though the country mouse was so full he could hardly move) strawberry cake and cream. The little mouse had never eaten such a fantastic feast!

Suddenly the door slammed and a bunch of noisy young men with two large dogs burst into the room. The terrified mice fled and hid under a cupboard, shaking with fear as the two dogs growled at them. Finally, when the men had gone to bed and the dogs had settled down to sleep, the country mouse crept out from his hiding place.

"Goodbye, cousin," he whispered. "This fine living is all very nice, but I would rather enjoy a crumb of bread in peace, than feast on this delicious food and live in constant fear."

Aesop's moral: It's better to enjoy bread and water in peace, than fine food in fear.

Time for Bed

As dusk fell over the jungle, the elephants huddled together and prepared to sleep. But Tootles the baby elephant wasn't ready for bed. He stomped around and drew patterns with his trunk in the dust.

"Come on, Tootles," smiled Mum. "It's time for bed."

Tootles tried to hide a yawn. "Can't we stay up and play?" he asked. "I don't want to go to sleep."

"Why not?" asked Mum. "You must be tired after such a long day."

"I don't want to say," said Tootles shyly. "You'll think I'm silly."

"I could never think you were silly," said Mum kindly. "Tell me what's troubling you."

Tootles looked up at his Mum and blushed. "I don't like the dark," he admitted. "Why does it have to be dark at bedtime? It makes me feel afraid."

Mum looked down at Tootles and smiled. "But the dark is a good thing," she said. "It's like a soft blanket covering the world, letting everyone know it's time to go to sleep."

"But I might have bad dreams," said Tootles, who was still not convinced.

"No, you won't," said Mum. "The world is full of good dreams, if you know where to find them. Look up at the sky."

So Tootles looked up at the night sky. It was a moonlit night, and the sky was full of twinkling stars.

"Each star is a good dream, just waiting for you," explained Mum. "And just look at how many there are!"

"Wow!" said Tootles. "There must be millions. I can't wait to go to sleep now... I wonder how many good dreams I will have tonight!"

Tootles began to count the stars, but before he got to ten, he was sound asleep.

Mum smiled down at him and wrapped her trunk around his warm body. **"Sweet dreams!"** she whispered.

Milly the Kangaroo

Milly was a kangaroo who loved to bounce and hop.
Every time she started – she didn't want to stop!
She bounced around all morning, and every afternoon.
She bounced around the forest, beside the blue lagoon.
"Look at me," she'd chuckle, bouncing to the sky.
"I'm a flying kangaroo, I can bounce so high!"
Milly never got fed up of bouncing up and down,
Even when she went to school or shopping in the town.
Her Mum would hop beside her and offer things to eat,
But Milly never stopped at all – not even for a treat.
And when she snuggled down at night
Beneath the moonlight's beams…
She just kept right on hopping by bouncing in her dreams!

Crocus the Crocodile

Crocus was a friendly crocodile who never, ever ate other animals. The problem was that no one else knew this.

"Hello!" he called to Antelope and Zebra, as he swam along the river. And he smiled his biggest, toothiest grin. But as soon as they saw him, Antelope and Zebra just hid in the bushes.

"How strange," thought Crocus as he waved to Wild Pig and her babies, and gave them his best smile.

"Eeeeeee!" squealed the little piglets, darting away.

Crocus began to cry. "No one wants to be my friend."

"You seem all right to me," said Hippo, who was passing by.

"Do I?" asked Crocus. And he gave Hippo his toothiest smile.

"Ahh," said Hippo. "Now I see the problem. They think you want to eat them with your big teeth."

"But I'm a vegetarian," shouted Crocus at the top of his voice. "I don't eat animals!"

His words echoed around the jungle and through the treetops.

"Did you hear that?" the other animals cried. "Crocus is a vegetarian! Let's make friends with him."

And that's exactly what they did. Of course, Crocus was very happy – but he tried his best not to smile about it too much!

The Cold Old House

I know a house, and a cold old house,
A cold old house by the sea.
If I were a mouse in that cold old house
What a cold, cold mouse I would be!

Who's That Ringing?

Who's that ringing at my door bell?
A little kitty cat that isn't very well.
Rub its nose with a little butter fat,
That's the best cure for a little kitty cat.

Young Lambs to Sell

Young lambs to sell!
Young lambs to sell!
If I'd as much money as I could tell,
I never would cry, young lambs to sell!

Small Is the Wren

Small is the wren,
Black is the rook,
Great is the thief
That steals this book!

To the Snail

Snail, snail,
put out your horns,
And I will give you
bread and barleycorns.

Two Young Pigs

I went to walk with two young pigs,
In satin vests and fancy wigs.
But suddenly it chanced to rain,
And so they all went home again.

Bertha the Goat

It was breakfast time, and Bertha the goat was very hungry.

"Maa," she called as the farmer walked into the barnyard with a bucket of food. But he walked right past Bertha and tipped the scraps into Pig's trough.

"Can I try some?" asked Bertha. And she gobbled up Pig's scraps before he could reply. She only stopped when she saw the farmer pouring milk into Cat's bowl.

"Can I try some?" asked Bertha. And she lapped up the milk before Cat could even reply.

By now Bertha was beginning to feel kind of full, but when she saw the farmer putting hay into Horse's manger she rushed over and she started munching before Horse could say a word.

Suddenly Bertha heard a familiar sound. The farmer was pouring nuts into her trough. Bertha groaned. She had eaten so much that her poor belly was full up and she couldn't eat another bite.

"Can we have some?" shouted all the other animals. "Some greedy goat gobbled down all our breakfasts."

Bertha looked shamefaced. "I promise not to be so greedy ever again," she promised.

Matty the Koala

"It's time for your nap," called Matty the baby koala's mum.

"But I'm not sleepy," said Matty. "I want to explore."

"Of course you're sleepy," laughed Mrs Koala. "Koalas are always sleepy. We can go exploring later." And she popped Matty into her pouch and curled up in the eucalyptus tree.

But Matty didn't want a nap – he wanted to explore. When he was sure his mum was asleep, he crept quietly out of her pouch, down the tree and scampered off into the forest.

High in the trees, he spotted a colourful parakeet.

"Yeeah!" he cried, chasing after it. Then he heard a funny sound. Ribbet! Matty looked around and saw a huge, warty toad puffing out its chest. It looked so funny that he giggled.

Suddenly Matty heard a scary sound. Hisssssssssss!

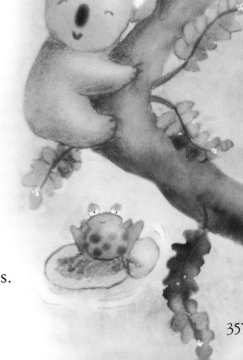

"It's a snake!" cried Matty.

The frightened little koala ran as fast as his legs would carry him back to the eucalyptus tree, and dived into his mum's pouch.

"Ooooooh," yawned Mrs Koala, smiling down at Matty. "Come on, sleepyhead. It's time to explore." But Matty didn't say a word. He was fast asleep after his adventures.

Bernie Becomes a Mum!

One day Bernie the drake went to visit Dilly the Duck. Dilly had been sitting on her eggs for weeks and was getting bored.

"Is there anything I can do to help?" asked Bernie.

"Well, since you've asked," said Dilly, "I'd love to go for a dip in the pond. Could you keep my eggs warm while I'm gone?"

"I'd be delighted," said Bernie. "But what happens if they hatch while you are away?"

"Don't worry. They won't," laughed Dilly. "They're not due to hatch until tomorrow."

"Okay," quacked Bernie. And he settled himself gently onto the eggs and made himself comfortable.

"Ah, this is easy," thought Bernie proudly, and he began to daydream about a brood of cute ducklings calling him Uncle Bernie. He was just dozing off to sleep when a loud CRACK awoke him.

All at once, the nest was full of cracking sounds.

"What's happening?" cried Bernie, trying hard not to panic.

Bernie got up and looked beneath him. A row of fluffy faces peered back. "Mamma!" quacked the little ducklings.

"I'm not your Mummy!" cried Bernie in alarm. But no matter how much he told them, the little ducklings didn't seem to hear. "Mamma! Mamma!" they quacked.

By the end of the morning, Bernie was at his wits' end.

"I'll have to find Dilly right away!" he decided.

Bernie leaped off the nest in a flurry of feathers and raced down to the pond. "Stay there," he yelled over his shoulder. But the little ducklings were much too young to understand.

"Mamma! Mamma!" they quacked, as they waddled after him and plopped into the water.

Bernie didn't know what to do, so he swam round and round in circles, herding the ducklings into a neat group. He was so busy that he didn't see Dilly until she popped up beside him. He hung his head in shame. He just knew that Dilly was going to be furious. But he was wrong.

"Oh, well done, Bernie!" she quacked. "Not only have you hatched my eggs – you've taught my ducklings to swim, too! What a good mum you are."

That's Not My Sister!

"Hey, Manny," said Molly. "Let's play hide-and-seek.
I'll hide while you count up to twenty. Don't peek!"
  So Manny stood counting, his eyes both shut tight,
as Molly ran into the trees out of sight.
  "Ready or not, here I come!"
  "Lost your sister? You'll easily find her," said Hare.
"I saw something dash through those trees over there.

  So off galloped Manny, deep into the wood...
till he came to a place where a big oak tree stood.
  In the leaves Manny spotted two eyes, big and bright.
  "I've found you! I've found you!" he yelled in delight.
But it was Owl.
  "That's not my sister!" cried Manny.
  "Lost your sister?" smiled Owl. "Well, I heard a strange sound
from that pile of old logs over there on the ground."

The log pile was huge. What a great place to hide!
And who was that hustling and bustling inside?

"Aha!" Manny cried. "Hey there, Molly, come out!
I've found you! I've found you! I spotted your snout!"

But it was Beaver.

"That's not my sister!" cried Manny.

"Lost your sister?" grinned Beaver as she gnawed on a stick.
"You'll catch her down there by the lake if you're quick!"

Down by the lakeside, behind a tall spruce,
stood a big, antlered creature – it must be a moose!

Manny crept silently up, then quickly cried...
"I've found you! I've found you, as easy as pie!"

But it was Grandpa.

"That's not my sister!" he cried.

"Lost your sister?" asked Grandpa. "You gave me a shock!
Run along now, and look over there by that rock."

At the rock Manny tried very hard to be brave,
when he heard something moving inside a dark cave.

He peered into the dark and said with a shout,
"I know you're in there! I've found you – come out!"
But it was Bear. **"You're not my sister!"**
"Lost your sister?" growled Bear, with his mouth full of honey.
"Have you checked in that grove over there, where it's sunny?"

In the bright, sunlit grove there was nothing to see...
but a huge pile of leaves lying under a tree.
Aha! What was that wriggling under the pile?
"I've found you! I've found you!" Manny cried with a smile.
But it was Porcupine.
"That's not my sister!"
cried Manny.

"Lost your sister?" asked Porcupine. "No room in here.

If she'd sat on me, she'd have yelled loud and clear!"

Then Manny saw a large creature run into some trees, and heard "AH–AH–CHOO!!!!" – an almighty sneeze!

"That's my sister!" cried Manny. And it was.

"It's my turn now," the happy moose cried. "You count to twenty while I go and hide!"

So Molly counted, "1–2–3…"

… while Manny ran off to hide with glee.

Manny stood still, without a sound… in a place he was sure that he'd never be found…

Let's Play Pirates

"Let's play Pirates!" Pippa said,
And everyone agreed.
So they're searching round the castle
To find the things they need.
1,2,3,4,5... searching everywhere,
Upstairs and downstairs.
Ooh, what's that over there?
"Here's 1 bathtub for a ship," says Pip.
"Now we need to get...
2 sticks to hold the sails up,
So we can't stop searching yet!"
1,2,3,4,5... searching everywhere,
Upstairs and downstairs.
Ooh, what's that over there?
Boris says, "We need 3 sails,
To make the ship go faster!"
So Pippa goes to search again,
But Boris pushes past her.

1,2,3,4,5... searching everywhere,
Upstairs and downstairs.
Ooh, what's that over there?
"Flags!" cries Little Dragon.
"I think we should have 4."
So everyone jumps up and hurries off
To search and find some more.
1,2,3,4,5... searching everywhere,
Upstairs and downstairs.
Ooh, what's that over there?
"Now we need 5 pirate hats,
And we can have some fun!"
But then the dinner trumpet sounds,
And off they have to run!

The Pigeon

A pigeon and a pigeon's son
Once went to town to buy a bun.
They couldn't decide on a plum or plain,
And so they flew back home again.

The Snail

The snail he lives in his hard round house,
In the orchard, under the tree:
Says he, "I have but a single room;
But it's large enough for me."

The Fuzzy Caterpillar

The fuzzy caterpillar
Curled up on a leaf,
Spun her little chrysalis
And then fell fast asleep.
While she was a-sleeping
She dreamed that she could fly,
And later when she woke up
She was a butterfly!

Cobweb Races

No wonder spiders wear bare feet
To run their cobweb races.
Suppose they had to have eight shoes,
How would they tie their laces?

Rabbits and Squirrels

Rabbits and squirrels are furry and fat,
And all of the chickens have feathers, and that
Is why when it's raining they need not stay in,
The way children do, who only have skin.

Ride Away, Ride Away

Ride away, ride away,
Johnny shall ride,
He shall have a kitty cat
Tied to one side;
He shall have a little dog
Tied to the other,
And Johnny shall ride
To see his grandmother.

Ten Little Pigs

Ten little pigs went to market,
One of them fell down,
and one of them ran away.
How many got to town?
Eight!

Eight little pigs went to market,
One of them fell down,
and one of them ran away.
How many got to town?
Six

Six little pigs went to market,
One of them fell down,
and one of them ran away.
How many got to town?
Four!

Four little pigs went to market,
One of them fell down,
and one of them ran away.
How many got to town?
Two!

Two little pigs went to market,
One of them fell down,
and one of them ran away.
How many got to town?
None!

The Wise Little Pig

Where are you going to, you little pig?
I'm leaving my mother, I'm growing so big!
So big, you young pig!
So young, so big!
What! leaving your mother, you foolish young pig?
Where are you going to, you little pig?
I've got a new spade, and I'm going to dig!
To dig, little pig!
A little pig dig!
Well, I never saw a pig with a spade that could dig!
Where are you going to, you little pig?
Why, I'm going to have a nice ride in a gig!
In a gig, little pig!
What! A pig in a gig!
Well, I never yet saw a pig in a gig!
Where are you going to, you little pig?
I'm going to the barber's to buy me a wig.
A wig, little pig!
A pig in a wig!
Why, whoever before saw a pig in a wig?
Where are you going to, you little pig?
I'm going to the ball to dance a fine jig!
A jig, little pig!
A pig dance a jig!
Well, I never before saw a pig dance a jig!

Little Beak

Little Beak lived on a mountaintop with his mum, dad and sister, Light Feather. One day Dad told him that it was time to learn to fly.

"But I can't fly," gulped Little Beak. "I'll fall."

"You can," said Mum. "You just need to flap your wings."

"I'll do it," cried Light Feather, throwing herself out of the nest and flapping her wings. Little Beak held his breath as Light Feather soared through the sky. "Come on," she called, swooping in circles. "It's easy!"

All of a sudden, Light Feather stopped flying and fell through the air. Little Beak cried out, but Mum and Dad were too far away to hear. He would have to do something! Bravely, he jumped out of the nest and flapped his wings. To his surprise, he began flying clumsily through the air. Looking around, he saw Light Feather just ahead. "But I saw you fall," he cried.

"I wasn't falling," she laughed. "I was hiding from you."

Little Beak was so angry that he began beating his wings quickly. Soon he was soaring past Light Feather. It felt wonderful.

"Come on, slowcoach," he called. "Flying is easy!"

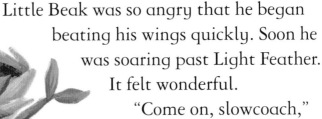

George's Itch

It was bedtime, but George the
raccoon had an itchy back and
couldn't sleep. He looked around
and spotted a prickly bush.

"Ahaaa! That'll do the trick!"
he cried, and began to rub his
back against the prickles.

"Do you mind?" said a bird
in the bush. "I'm trying to sleep."

"Sorry," whispered George.
He looked around and picked up a stick.
He was just about to scratch his back with it when the stick
began to hiss. It was an angry snake!

"Do you mind?" hissed the snake. "I'm trying to sleep."

"Sorry," whispered George. He wandered around until he
reached a big, bumpy hill. "Sliding over those bumps is sure
to get rid of my itch," he thought. So he climbed to the top
and began to slide down. Faster and faster he slid, until he
was tumbling out of control. He didn't stop until he thumped
BUMP! into Rabbit, who was curled up asleep in the roots
of the tree at the bottom of the hill.

"Whatever are you up to?" asked Rabbit, rubbing his head.

"I'm trying to get rid of an itch on my back," said George.

"Next time, just ask me," laughed Rabbit, reaching over to
scratch George's tricky itch. "Then we can all get some sleep!"

Chester the Squirrel

It was a cold winter day and
Chester the squirrel was feeling
even grumpier than normal.
It had started snowing the night
before, and now the forest was
covered in a thick, white blanket.

"Horrible cold stuff," he
grumbled, as he watched the other
animals having a snowball fight
outside. "Just look at those silly
creatures getting cold and tired.
I'll stay inside and have a feast in front of my warm fire.
But first I've got something to do."

Chester got out some paper and wrote a sign in his best
handwriting. Then he pinned it on his door. The sign read:

NO SNOWBALL FIGHTING HERE – or else!

"That should frighten them away," smiled Chester, going
back inside to prepare his feast. But when he opened his
pantry, he gave a shriek of surprise. The shelves were bare!
There was not a single nut left. He had completely forgotten
that he had eaten his last nut the night before.

"Oh, no," thought Chester. "I'll have to venture out into the nasty snow and get some more nuts from my secret hiding place. But what if the other animals follow me and find out where I keep them? There's no way I'm going to share with that greedy bunch."

So Chester waited until he was sure the coast was clear. Then he put on his warm scarf and ventured out into the snow.

"Brrrrr!" he shivered as he hurried through the chilly evening. "I really can't see the point of snow. It's just a nuisance."

Chester hadn't gone far before he heard the pitter-patter of tiny feet behind him. "Someone must be following me," he thought. And he hid behind some tree roots to see who it was.

Chester frowned as Timmy Dormouse trotted by. Timmy was whistling and looking very pleased with himself. And he was heading straight toward the Big Elm where Chester's secret supply of nuts was hidden.

"Oh, no, you don't," cried Chester, leaping out from his hiding place. But he didn't get far, because his foot got tangled up in the roots.

"Ahhhh," squealed Chester, as he fell to the ground with a heavy THUD! He groaned and moved his leg. But he was quite surprised to discover that he hadn't hurt himself one bit.

"That's strange," he muttered.

"I don't seem to have hurt myself at all."

"That's because the snow has given you a soft landing," said Timmy Dormouse, helping Chester to his feet.

"So it has," agreed Chester. "Maybe snow isn't all bad, after all."

"Of course it's not," laughed Timmy. "Snow is great. You can sledge on it, slide in it..." Timmy slid through the snow to demonstrate. "You can make snowmen out of it."

He pointed to some figures he and his friends had built.

"And…" he picked up a ball of snow and threw it gently at Chester's round belly, "… best of all, you can have snowball fights with it."

Chester looked so shocked that Timmy thought he was going to yell at him. But then his lips began to twitch and he started to laugh. He picked up a ball of snow of his own and threw it at Timmy. Soon they were having a noisy snowball fight. Chester had never had so much fun. When they had finished enjoying themselves, Chester felt so happy that he showed

Timmy his secret supply of nuts.

"Oh, we all know about your secret store," smiled Timmy.

Chester looked confused. "Well if you all know about it, why haven't you taken my nuts?"

Timmy looked startled. "Because they belong to you, of course," he said in surprise. "No forest animal would take something that didn't belong to them. What a terrible thing to think."

Chester looked suitably shamefaced. Then he had an idea. He rushed to his supply, grabbed a sack of nuts, and handed it to Timmy. He knew that Timmy and his family always went hungry during the winter months. "Here," he said. "Take these home and have a feast."

Timmy was delighted. "Thank you," he cried. "Why don't you come out and play with us in the snow tomorrow?"

"I will," said Chester. "But I've got something to do first."

Chester rushed home and took down the sign on his door.

He got out his pen and made some quick changes.

N̶O̶ SNOWBALL
FIGHTING HERE
at 12 – o̶r̶ ̶e̶l̶s̶e̶
Followed by nut
feast!

Shoe the Horse

Shoe the horse and shoe the mare,
But let the little colt go bare.

When I Was a Little Boy

When I was a little boy,
I washed my mother's dishes.
I put my finger in my ear,
And pulled out little fishes.
My mother called me good boy,
And bid me pull out more.
I put my finger in my ear,
And pulled out four score.

Three Ducks in a Brook

Look, look, look!
Three ducks in a brook.
One is white, and one is brown.
One is swimming upside down.
Look, look, look!
Three ducks in a brook.

There Was a Rat

There was a rat, for want of stairs,
Went down a rope to say his prayers.

A Dog and a Cat

A dog and a cat went out together,
To see some friends just out of town;
Said the cat to the dog,
"What d'ye think of the weather?"
"I think, Ma'am, the rain will come down.
But don't be alarmed, for I've an umbrella
That will shelter us both,"
Said this amiable fella.

The Wise Old Owl

The wise old owl
Sat on a branch,
His big round eyes shut tight.
"Tu whit, tu whoo,"
He softly called.
"Tu whit, tu whoo!
Goodnight!"

Little Dragon Goes Fishing

Little Dragon was fishing. He dipped his net in the pond and swished it around.

"I've caught a fish!" he cried. But he hadn't caught a fish at all. He had caught a red rubber boot.

"One boot is not much use on its own," said Little Dragon. "I need to catch the other one too."

He was just about to dip the net in the water again when along came his friends, Princess Pippa, Prince Pip and Baron Boris.

"What are you doing?" they asked.

"I'm catching red rubber boots," said Little Dragon. "Do you want to take a turn?"

"Yes, please!" said Princess Pippa. "I've always wanted a pair of red boots."

Princess Pippa swished the net around in the pond, and pulled out... a yellow umbrella.

"I wasn't expecting that!" she said.

Prince Pip took a turn with the
fishing net too.

"I've caught something heavy!"
he called. He heaved the net out
of the water.

"It's... a blue bucket full of holes!"
Baron Boris grabbed the net.

"It's my turn now!" he said.
"I'm going to catch something
much better than that."

Baron Boris spotted something under a lily pad.

"A green fish!" he cried. And he leaned forward to scoop it up.

Oh, dear! It wasn't a green fish at all. It was a green frog...
and an angry one, too!

"Ribbet!" it croaked, leaping out of the net. Baron Boris
was so scared that he fell into the water with a SPLASH!

"I think we will need a much bigger net to catch Baron
Boris!" said Little Dragon.

The Chipmunk and the Bear

One day a bear was walking through the woods.

"I am so strong, I can do anything," he shouted out proudly, lifting up tree trunks with one paw to search for food.

"Not anything!" said a small voice.

The bear looked down at the ground and saw a chipmunk with his head sticking out of a hole.

"You can't stop the sun from rising," the chipmunk said.

"I'm sure I could," boasted the bear. "In fact, I will do it tomorrow. Tomorrow the sun will not come up!"

So the bear and the chipmunk sat side by side all night,

facing the east, waiting to see if the sun would rise.

"The sun will not come up," the bear chanted.

"The sun will come up," the chipmunk chanted, but very quietly under his breath.

As morning approached, the sky began to lighten.

"The sun will not come up. I command it!" the bear shouted.

Slowly, the sun began to appear, and the chipmunk started to laugh.

"The sun has made a fool of you!" he taunted.

The bear was furious. His paw shot out and pinned the chipmunk to the ground.

"We'll see who the biggest fool is now!" he growled.

The chipmunk realised he had made a big mistake and should not have teased the bear.

"I am sorry," he squeaked. "You are right! I am worthless, and you are one of the greatest and strongest animals in the world. Please just lift your paw so I can catch my breath to tell you how much I admire you."

The bear was very vain, so he raised his paw a little. Quick as a flash, the chipmunk darted away, but as he escaped, the bear's claws scratched his back. And, to this day, the chipmunk still carries the claw marks on his back as a reminder to think twice before making fun of someone.

Index